2/20/00

To my dear frien[d]
    MacKenzie,

    I hope you enjoy read[ing]
this book and that it
encourages you to seek
our God and His path for
your life even more.

        My love to you —
    since the day you
        were born,

            Lana Mitchell

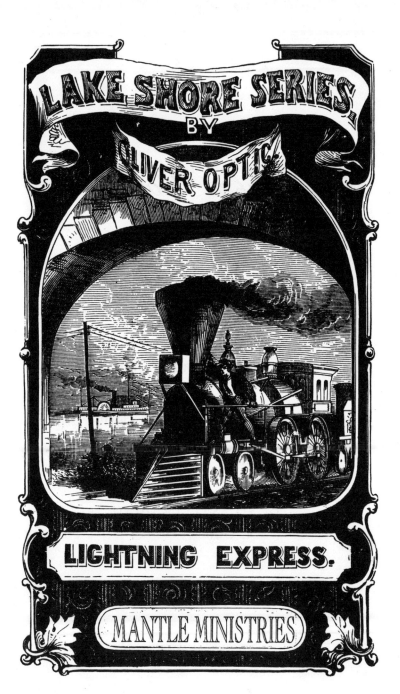

The Lake Shore Series

THROUGH
BY
DAYLIGHT
Or, The Young Engineer

By
OLIVER OPTIC

Illustrated

Published in 1869 Re-published 1998
(Protected)

Mantle Ministries
228 Still Ridge
Bulverde, Texas 78163
Ph 1-830-438-3777
Web http//www.mantlemin.com
E-Mail: mantle3377@aol.com

William T. Adams

About the Author

William Taylor Adams was born in Boston in 1822. Prior to becoming a successful writer, he taught school, but found he could have far greater influence upon the youth of America by writing books and short stories for magazines. Mr Adams' name does not appear on his stories for he adopted "Oliver Optic" as a pen name, which immediately found favor across this nation. By 1867 he was publishing a magazine called *Oliver Optic's Magazine for Boys and Girls.*

Little did Mr. Adams realize just how the Lord was going to crown his success. By the time of his death in 1897, at the age of 75, he had written more than 1,000 short stories and more than 115 novels, the majority of which portray youthful heroes and heroines of noble, self-sacrificing, courageous and moral character, challenged by adverse circumstances. Each adventure weaves the thread of Biblical principles throughout the stirring plots with inspirational design.

The following is his personal testimony in regard to his faith in Christ, documented by Dr. Stephen Abbott Northrop on page 4 of his 1899 classic book, *A Cloud Of Witnesses*

"I was a constant church-goer for fifty years until my hearing failed me, so that I do not attend divine services or meetings of any kind. I was connected with the Sunday-school for twenty years.

I regard Jesus Christ as the purest and holiest Being ever on earth, and whose teachings, ministry, and example have been "the Light of the World. I look upon the Bible as the greatest and best Book ever given to man, especially the New Testament, which contains the Life and the Word of our Lord and Saviour."

PREFACE.

The Lake Shore Series, of which this book is the first volume, includes six stories, whose locality and principal characters are nearly the same, and which were originally published in Oliver Optic's Magazine, Our Boys and Girls. The railroad, which is the basis of the incidents in the first and second volumes, was suggested by the experience of several young gentlemen in Ohio, who had formed a company, and transacted all the business of a railroad in regular form, for the purpose of obtaining a practical knowledge of the details of such a corporation. They issued certificates of shares, bonds, with interest coupons, elected officers, and appointed all the employees required for the management of a well-ordered railroad. The author is the fortunate possessor of one of the bonds of this company — "The Miami Valley Railroad."

The young engineer is doubtless a smart boy; but so far as his mechanical skill is concerned, several counterparts of him have come to the knowledge of the writer. If he has an "old head," he has a young heart, which he endeavors to keep pure and true. As he appears in this and the subsequent volumes of the series, the author is willing to commend him as an example of the moral and Christian hero, who cannot lead his imitators astray; for he loves truth and goodness, and is willing to forgive and serve his enemies.

HARRISON SQUARE, MASS.,

July 21, 1869.

CONTENTS.

CHAPTER VIII.

CHAPTER IX.

CHAPTER X.

CHAPTER XI.

CHAPTER XII.

CHAPTER XIII.

CHAPTER XIV.

CHAPTER XV.

CHAPTER XVI.

CHAPTER XVII.

CHAPTER XVIII.

CHAPTER XIX.

CHAPTER XX.

CHAPTER XXI.

CHAPTER XXII.

CHAPTER XXIII.

CHAPTER XXIV.

CHAPTER XXV.

CHAPTER XXVI.

Contents

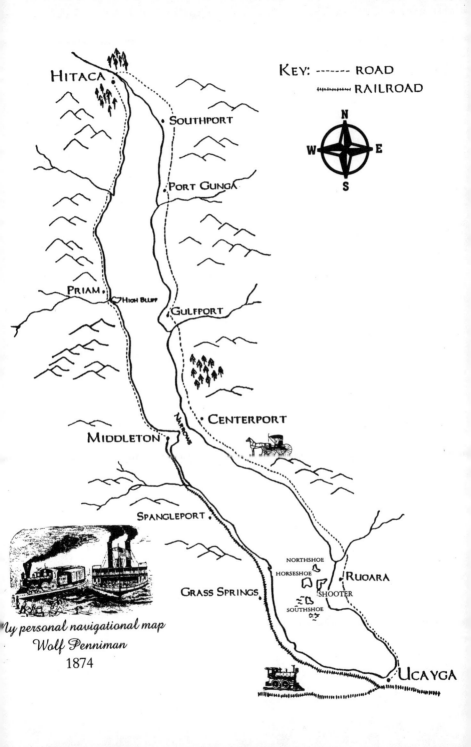

KEY: ------ ROAD
〜〜〜〜 RAILROAD

N
W E
S

HITACA

SOUTHPORT

PORT GUNGA

PRIAM

High Bluff

GULFPORT

NARROWS

CENTERPORT

MIDDLETON

SPANGLEPORT

NORTHSHOE

HORSESHOE

SHOOTER

RUOARA

GRASS SPRINGS

SOUTHSHOE

My personal navigational map
Wolf Penniman
1874

UCAYGA

THROUGH BY DAYLIGHT;

OR,

THE YOUNG ENGINEER OF THE LAKE-SHORE RAILROAD.

————————◆————————

CHAPTER I.

MR. WADDIE WIMPLETON.

POP, pop, pop, pop, pop, pop — six pops.

Mr. Waddie Wimpleton, an elegant young gentleman of fifteen, by all odds the nicest young man in Centreport, was firing at a mark with a revolver. It was a very beautiful revolver, too, silver-mounted, richly chased, and highly polished in all its parts, discharging six shots at each revolution, not often at the target, in the unskilful hands of Mr. Waddie, but sometimes near enough to indicate what the marksman was shooting at.

Even the target was quite an elaborate affair; and

11

though Mr. Waddie had been shooting at it for a week, it was hardly damaged by the trial to which it had been subjected. It was two feet in diameter, having in its centre a tolerably correct resemblance of one of the optics of a bovine masculine; and this enigma, being literally interpreted, meant the bull's eye, which Mr. Waddie was expected to hit, or at least to try to hit. Around it were several circles in black, red, yellow, green, and blue, each indicating a certain distance from the objective point of the shooter. There were a few holes in the target within these circles, but the central eye was not put out, and still glared defiance at the ambitious marksman.

Mr. Waddie Wimpleton had everything he wanted, and therefore never wanted anything he had. There was no end to the ponies, sail-boats, row-boats, guns, pistols, fishing-rods, and other sporting gear, which came into his possession, and of which he soon became weary. His father was as rich as an East-Indian prince, and Mr. Waddie being an only son, though there were two daughters who partially " put his nose out of joint," his paternal parent had labored industriously to spoil the child from babyhood. I am forced to acknowledge that he succeeded even better than he intended.

Mr. Waddie was always waiting and watching for a new sensation. A magnificent kite, of party-colored silk, had evidently occupied his attention during the earlier hours of the morning, and it now lay neglected on the ground, the line stretched off in the direction of the lake. The young gentleman had become tired of the plaything, and when I approached him he was blazing away at the target with the revolver, at the rate of six shots in three seconds. I halted at a respectful distance from the marksman. He was not shooting at me, but I regarded this as the very reason why he would be likely to hit me. If he had been aiming at me, I should have approached him with more confidence.

Keeping well in the rear of the young gentleman, I came within hailing distance of him. I did not belong to the "upper-ten" of Centreport, and I could not be said to be familiarly acquainted with him. My father was the engineer in his father's steam-flouring mills, and a person of my humble connections was of no account in his estimation. But I am

forced to confess that I had not that awe and respect for Mr. Waddie which wealth and a lofty social
position demand of the humble classes. I had the
audacity to approach the young scion of an influential house; and it was audacious, considered in
reference to his pistol, if not to his social position.

Pop, pop, pop, went the revolver again, as I placed
myself about five rods in his rear, feeling tolerably
safe in this position. When he had fired the three
shots, he stopped and looked at me. I could not
help noticing that his face wore an unusual aspect.
Though he was at play, engaged in what would have
been exceedingly exciting sport to a boy of my
simple tastes, he did not appear to enjoy it. To be
entirely candid, he looked ugly, and seemed to have
no interest whatever in his game.

Mr. Waddie Wimpleton could not only look ugly,
but he could be ugly — as ugly as sin itself. Only
the day before he had been concerned in an awful
row on board of a canal boat, which lay at the pier
a dozen rods from the spot where he was shooting.
The boat had brought down a load of coal for the
use of the steam mill, and, having discharged her

cargo, was waiting till a fleet should be gathered of sufficient numbers to employ a small steamer to tow them up the lake. Mr. Waddie had gone on board. The owner's family, according to the custom, lived in the cabin, and the young gentleman had employed his leisure moments in teasing the skipper's daughter, a pretty and spirited girl of his own age. She answered his taunting speech with so much vim that Mr. Waddie got mad, and absolutely insulted her, using language which no gentleman would use in the presence of a female.

At this point her father interfered, and reproved the nice young man so sharply, and withal so justly, that Waddie's wrath turned from the daughter to the parent, and in his anger he picked up a piece of coal and hurled it at the honest skipper's head. The latter, being the independent owner and master of the canal boat, and also an American citizen with certain unalienable rights, dodged the missile, and resented the impudence by seizing the young scion of an influential house by the collar of his coat, and after giving him a thorough shaking, much to the discomfiture of his purple and fine linen, threw him on the pier, very much as a Scotch terrier disposes of a rat after he has sufficiently mauled him.

Mr. Waddie was not accustomed to this sort of treatment. Whatever he did in Centreport, and especially about his father's estate and the steam mills, no one thought of opposing him. If he set any one's shed on fire, shot anybody's cow, or did other mischief, the only remedy was to carry a bill of damages to the young gentleman's father; and then, though the claim was for double the value of the cow or the shed, the fond parent paid it without murmuring. No one had ever thought of taking satisfaction for injuries by laying violent hands on the scion.

But the worthy captain of the canal boat, though he knew Colonel Wimpleton very well, had not learned to appraise an insult to him or his family in dollars and cents. The "young rascal," as he profanely called the young gentleman, had insulted his daughter, had used vile and unbecoming language to her, and, if he had had a cowhide in his hand at the time, he would have used it unmercifully upon the soft skin of the dainty scion. He had no weapon but in his strong arms. Mr. Waddie had been made to feel the weight of his muscle, and to see more stars than often twinkled over the tranquil surface of Lake Ucayga.

Perhaps, if the indignant skipper of the canal boat had known Mr. Waddie better, he would have been disposed to moderate his wrath, and to have chosen a less objectionable mode of chastising his victim; though on this point I am not clear, for he was an American citizen, and an unprovoked insult to his daughter was more than he could patiently endure.

Mr. Waddie struck the pier on his "beam ends." I beg to inform my readers that I am a fresh-water sailor, and from the force of habit sometimes indulge in salt expressions. In the rapid evolutions which he had been compelled to make under the energetic treatment of the stalwart skipper, his ideas were considerably "mixed." His body had performed so many unwonted and involuntary gyrations, that his muscles and limbs had been twisted into an aching condition. Besides, he struck the planks, whereof the pier was composed, so heavily, that the shock jounced from his body almost all the breath which had not been ex-

2

pended in the gust of passion preceding the final catastrophe.

The scion lay on the pier like a branch detached from the parent tree; for if he realized anything in that moment of defeat and disaster, it was that not even his father's influence had, on this occasion, saved him from deserved retribution. He must have felt for the instant like one alone in the world. Mr. Waddie was ugly, as I have before suggested. The dose which had just been administered to him needed to be repeated many times, in order to effect a radical cure of his besetting sin. He was well punished, but unfortunately his antecedents had not been such as to prepare him for the remedial agency. It did him no good.

Mr. Waddie lay upon the pier roaring like a bull. According to the legends of his childhood, some one ought to come and pick him up; some one ought to appear and mollify his rage, by promising summary vengeance upon the " naughty man " who had upset his philosophy, and almost riven his joints asunder. But no one came. His father and mother were not within the hearing of his voice — no one but myself and the irate skipper and his family. The young gentleman lay on the pier and roared. All the traditions of the past were falsified, for no one came to his aid. I did not consider it my duty to meddle, under the circumstances, and the skipper would sooner have shaken him again than undone the good deed he had accomplished.

As no one came to comfort him, Mr. Waddie roared till he was tired of roaring — till the breath came back to his body, and the full measure of ugliness came back to his mind. He got up. He walked down to the side of the canal boat, where the honest captain was sitting composedly on his stool. Mr. Waddie stormed furiously; Mr. Waddie even swore violently. Mr. Waddie inquired, in heated terms, if the honest skipper knew who he was.

The honest skipper did not care who he was. He was an "unlicked cub." No man or boy should insult his "darter" without as heavy a thrashing as he felt able to give him; and if the young gentleman gave him any more "sarse," he would just step ashore and dip him a few times in the lake, just by way of cooling his heated blood, and giving him a lesson in good manners.

Mr. Waddie had already tasted the quality of the skipper's muscle, and he slowly retreated from the pier; but as he went, he vowed vengeance upon the author of his disaster. As he passed the spot where I was stopping a leak in an old skiff belonging to my father, he repeated his threats, and I felt confident at the time that Mr. Waddie intended to annihilate the honest skipper at the first convenient opportunity.

CHAPTER II.

A TREMENDOUS EXPLOSION.

MR. WADDIE fired three shots from his revolver, and then turned to look at me; and he looked ugly.

My father's house was near the spot. I had been planting peas in the garden all the morning, and I had observed that the young gentleman was unusually steadfast in his occupations. He had raised his kite, and kept it up for half an hour. Then he had fastened the string to the target, and "run it down." Occasionally I glanced at him to see what he was about. After he had brought the kite down, I saw him bringing it up to the target. Then he went on board of the canal boat at the pier. The honest skipper had locked up the cabin, and gone with his family to visit his relations at Ruoara, eight miles below Centreport.

Mr. Waddie appeared to be making himself at home on board. He went down into the hold, and remained there a considerable time. After the savage threats I had heard him make the day before, it would not have surprised me to see the flames rising from the honest skipper's craft; but nothing of this kind had yet occurred, though I was fully satisfied that the scion was plotting mischief. After he had been on board half an hour, he returned to the target and popped away a while at it, though, as I have before observed, he did not seem to take any particular interest in the amusement.

On this day the flour mills were not at work, having suspended operations to put in a new boiler. After everything was ready for it the boiler did not arrive, and all hands were obliged to take a vacation, to await its coming. The mill was, therefore, deserted, and my father had a little time to attend to his own affairs. He was going down to Ucayga, at the foot of the lake, upon business, which I shall have occasion to explain by and by. He had gone up to the town, and as he had given me permission to go with him, I was to meet him at the steamboat landing. I was on my way to this point when I paused to observe Mr. Waddie's shooting.

A revolver is a very pretty toy for a boy of fifteen. My father would as soon have thought of giving me a live rattlesnake for a pet, as a pistol for a plaything. At the same time, I understood and appreciated the instrument, and should have been proud and happy as the possessor of it. Mr. Waddie, in one of his gracious moments, had permitted me to fire this pistol, and I flattered myself that I could handle it much better than he. He never did anything well, and therefore he did not shoot well. As I stood there, at a respectful distance, admiring the splendid weapon, I envied him the fun which might be got out of it, though I was very sure he did not make the most of it.

He suspended his operations, and looked at me. I hoped he was going to give me an invitation to shoot; and I felt that, if he did, I could soon spoil the enigmatical eye that glared at the shooter from the target.

"What do you want, Wolf?" said he.

Perhaps it is not necessary for me to explain that

I was not actually a wolf; but it is necessary for me to say that this savage appellation was the name by which I was usually known and called in Centreport. My father's name was Ralph Penniman, and at the time I was born he lived on the banks of the Hudson. He had taken such a strong fancy for some of the creations of Washington Irving, that he insisted, in spite of an earnest protest on the part of my mother, upon calling me Wolfert, after one of the distinguished author's well-known characters, who obtained a great deal of money where he least expected to find it. In vain my mother pleaded that the only possible nickname — in a land where nicknames were as inevitable as the baby's teeth — would be Wolf. My father continued to insist, having no particular objection to the odious name. I was called Wolfert, and I shall be Wolf as long as I live, — perhaps after I die, if the width of my tomb-stone compels the lapidary to abbreviate my name.

"What do you want, Wolf?" asked Mr. Waddie in a surly tone, which led me to think that I was an intruder.

"Nothing," I replied; and knowing how easy it was to get up a quarrel with the scion, I began to move on.

"Come here; I want you," added Mr. Waddie, in a tone which seemed to leave no alternative but obedience.

"I can't. I have to go to the steamboat wharf," I ventured to suggest.

"Oh, come here — will you? I won't keep you but a minute."

Mr. Waddie was almost invariably imperious; but now he used a coaxing tone, which I could not resist. I could not help seeing that there was some-thing about him which was strange and unnatural — a forced expression and manner, that it bothered me to explain. If the young gentleman was en-gaged in any mischief, he was sufficiently accus-tomed to it to do without any of the embarrassment which distinguished his present demeanor. But I could not see anything wrong, and he did not ap-pear to be engaged in any conspiracy against the canal boat, or the honest skipper in command of it. Appearances, however, are often delusive, and they could hardly be otherwise when Mr. Waddie attempted to look amiable and conciliatory.

"You are a good fellow, Wolf," he added.

I knew that before, and the intelligence was no news to me; yet the condescension of the scion was marvellous in the extreme, and I wondered what was going to happen, quite sure that something extraordinary was about to transpire.

"What do you want of me, Waddie?" I asked, curiously.

"I'm going up to the steamboat wharf, and I want you to help me wind up my kite-line," he added, bustling about as though he meant what he said.

"How came your kite-line over there when your kite is up here?"

"Oh, I untied it, and brought it up here so as not to tear the kite — that's all. Take hold of the string and pull it in."

I picked up the line. As I did so, Mr. Waddie gave a kind of a start, and held his elbow up at the side of his head. But I did not pull on the line, for, to tell the honest truth, I was afraid he was up to some trick.

"Why don't you haul it in, you fool?" demanded Waddie, with more excitement than the occasion seemed to require.

"I can't stop to wind it up, Waddie; I'm in a hurry. My father is waiting for me up at the wharf."

"It won't take but a couple of minutes; pull in, and I'll give you three shots with this revolver," he added.

"I can't stay to fire the shots now."

"Yes, you can! Come, pull in, and don't be all day about it," continued he, impatiently.

I was almost sure he was up to some trick; he was earnest and excited. The longer I stayed, the worse it would be for me, and I dropped the string.

"Pick it up again!" shouted Waddie; and at the same moment he fired off the pistol.

I did pick it up; for though the pistol ball did not come very near me, I heard it whistle through the air, and as I had never been under fire, I am willing to confess that it frightened me. I do not think Waddie meant to hit me when he fired, but this consciousness made me all the more fearful for my own safety.

"Now, pull in, you ninny! If you don't mind when your betters speak to you, I'll put one of these bullets into you."

"Do you mean to kill me, Waddie?" I asked.

"No, not if you mind what I say to you."

"But I tell you my father is waiting for me at the steamboat wharf."

"No matter if he is; he's paid for waiting when I want you. Why don't you pull in?"

I don't know exactly why I did not pull in. He threatened to shoot me, on the one hand, if I didn't pull in, and I felt as though something would happen, on the other hand, if I did pull in. It was not improbable to me, just then, that the young scion had planted a torpedo in the ground, which was to be touched off by pulling the string, and which was to send me flying up into the air. I would have given something handsome, at that moment, for ten rods of space between me and the imperative young scion at my side.

"Why don't you pull?" yelled he, out of patience with me at last.

Springing forward, he grasped the string which I

then held in my hand, and gave it a smart jerk, at the same time pointing the revolver at my head, as if to prevent my sudden departure. The pulling of the kite-string more than realized my expectations. The very earth was shaken beneath me, and the lake trembled under the shock that followed. High in air, from the pier, a dozen rods distant, rose, in ten thousand fragments, the canal boat of the honest skipper. By some trickery, which I could not understand, the gaily-painted craft had been blown up by the pulling of that kite-string.

I could not see through it; in fact, I was so utterly confounded by the noise, smoke, and dust of the explosion, that I did not try to see through it. I was amazed and confused, bewildered and paralyzed. The fragments of the boat had been scattered in a shower upon us, but none of them were large enough to do us any serious injury.

My first thought was a sentiment of admiration at the diabolical ingenuity of Mr. Waddie. It was clear enough now that this was the revenge of the young gentleman upon the skipper for the punishment he had inflicted upon him. By some contrivance, not yet explained, the young reprobate had ignited a quantity of powder, placed in the hold of the boat, with the kite-line. The honest skipper seemed to be the victim now.

"Now see what you have done!" exclaimed Mr. Waddie, when he, as well as I, had in some measure recovered from the shock.

"I didn't do it," I replied, indignantly.

"Yes, you did, you fool! Didn't you pull the string?"

"Not much! You pulled it yourself," I protested.

"At any rate, we are both of us in a very sweet scrape."

"I'm not in it; I didn't know anything about it, and I'm not going to stay here any longer," I retorted, moving off.

"Stop, Wolf!"

He pointed the pistol at me again. I had had about enough of this sort of thing, and I walked back to him.

"Now, Wolf, if you want to" —

I did not wait for him to say any more. Choos-

THE EXPLOSION.   Page 30.

ing my time, I sprang upon him, wrested the pistol
from his grasp, threw him over backwards, and
made good my retreat to a grove near the spot,
just as the people were hurrying down to ascertain
the cause of the explosion.

CHAPTER III.

WOLF'S FATHER.

THE grove into which I had retreated was on the border of Colonel Wimpleton's estate, and in its friendly covert I made my way to the road which led to the steamboat wharf. I put the pistol into my breast pocket, intending, of course, to give it back to Waddie when I saw him again. Just then I heard the whistle of the steamer, and hastened to the pier.

I was now far enough away from the scene of the explosion to be out of the reach of suspicious circumstances, and I had an opportunity to consider my relations to the startling event which had just transpired. I could not make up my mind whether Mr. Waddie had been afraid to pull the string which was to produce the blow-up, or whether he wished to implicate me in the affair. If he had not been utterly wanting in all the principles of boy-honor, I should not have suspected him of the latter. I could not attribute his conduct to a lack of brute courage, for he had finally pulled the string, though it was in my hands at the time he did so. But it was of no great consequence what his motives were. I had taken no part in the blowing up of the honest skipper's boat, and did not know what the programme was until the explosion came off. I felt that I was all right, therefore, especially as I had escaped from the spot without being seen by any one.

After the catastrophe had occurred, Waddie had rudely asked me to see what I had done. I had taken the trouble to deny my own personal agency in the affair, but he had finally insisted that I pulled the string. This indicated a purpose on his part. I was in some manner mixed up in the matter; but, as I had no grudge against the honest skipper, I could not see why any person should be willing to believe Waddie, even if he did declare that I was engaged in the mischief. But above and beyond all other considerations, I felt that I was not guilty, and it was not proper that an honest young man like me should bother his head about contingencies, and situations, and suspicions. It was enough to be free from guilt, and I was content to let the appearances take care of themselves.

I found my father on the pier when I arrived. He was dressed in his best clothes, and looked like the solid, substantial man that he was. He could not very well be genteel in his appearance, for the smoke and oil of his occupation clung to him, even when he wore his holiday suit. I have noticed that men of his calling — and my own for some years — find it almost if not quite impossible to get rid of a certain professional aspect which clings to them. I have almost always been able to tell an engineer when I see one. There is something in the calling which goes with the man wherever he goes.

Though my father was not, and could not be, genteel, I was not ashamed of him. On the contrary, I was very proud of him, and proud of the professional aspect he wore. His look and manner had a savor of engines and machinery, which I tried to obtain for myself. When I was going to have any new clothes, I always insisted that they should be blue, because my father never wore any other color; and I used to think, though I had not yet been thoroughly steeped in oil and smoke, that I was not very unlike an engineer.

Having acknowledged the possession of this pride of occupation, I ought to explain where I got it. It was not a mere vanity with me, for I desired to look like an engineer because I was one. My father and mother had been good parents to me, and had proper notions in regard to my present and future welfare. I was sixteen years old, and had been at school all the time, summer and winter, until the spring of the year in which my story opens. I do not like to be egotistical, but I must say — since there is no one else to say it for me — that I was considered a very good scholar. I had just graduated at the Wimpleton Institute, where I had taken a high rank. I had particularly distinguished myself in natural philosophy and chemistry, because these studies were nearer to my heart than any other.

I was my father's only boy, and he had always manifested a peculiar interest in me. Even before

I was old enough to go to school, while we lived on the banks of the Hudson, my father was in the habit of taking me into the engine-room with him. I used to ask him hundreds of childish questions about the machinery, whose answers I was not old enough to understand; but, as I grew in years and mental power, the questions were repeated, and so carefully explained, that, before I ever read a description of the steam-engine, I had a very tolerable idea of the principles upon which it was constructed, and knew its mechanical structure.

When I was old enough to read and understand books, the steam-engine became the study of my life. I not only studied its philosophy in school, but my father had quite a little library of books relating to the subject, which I had read a great many times, and whose contents I had considered with the utmost care. A large portion of my spare time was spent in the engine-room at the mills. I had even run the machine for a week when my father was sick.

I had gone farther than this in the study of my favorite theme. As an engineer, my father was well acquainted with all of the men of the same calling in the steamboats on the lake, and with some of them on the locomotives which ran on the railroad through Ucayga, at the foot of the lake. When our family paid a visit to our former residence on the Hudson, I rode on the engine all the way, and made a practical study of the locomotive. I flattered myself I could run the machine as well as the best of them. Christy Holgate was the engineer of the steamer now coming up to the pier, and under his instruction I had mastered the mysteries of the marine engine, with which I was already acquainted in theory, after much study of the subject in the books.

I did not pretend to know anything but the steam-engine, and I thought I understood that pretty well. My father thought so too, which very much strengthened my confidence in my own ability. I am sorry I have not some one else to tell my story for me, for it is very disagreeable to feel obliged to say so much about myself. I hope my friends will not think ill of me on this account, for they will see that I can't help saying it, for my story would seem monstrously impossible without this explanation.

"Wolf, what was that noise down by the mill, a little while ago?" asked my father, as I joined him at the wharf.

"The canal boat at the mill pier was blown up," I replied, with some embarrassment.

"Blown up!" exclaimed he.

"Yes, sir."

"They were blowing rocks back of the mill, and I thought they must have set off a seam-blast; but the noise did not seem to be in the direction of the quarry. I don't see how the canal boat could have blown up. It wasn't the water that blew her up. Do you know anything about it, Wolf?"

"Yes, sir; I know a good deal more about it than I wish I did," I answered, for my father had always been fair and square with me, and I should as soon have thought of cutting off my own nose as telling him a falsehood.

"What do you know, Wolf?" he asked, with a look which betokened a rather painful interest in the nature of the answer. "I hope there wan't any mischief about it."

"It was all mischief."

"Who did it ? Not you, I hope."

"No, sir; I did not know anything about it till the boat blew up. Waddie Wimpleton did it."

"Of course he did," said my father, nodding his head significantly. "Did you see him do it?"

In reply I told the whole story, after we had gone on board of the steamer, giving every particular as minutely as though I had been a witness in a murder trial.

"I heard Waddie had had a row with the captain of the canal boat," added my father, who seemed to be vexed and disturbed more than I thought the occasion required, as he could not but see that I had no guilty knowledge of the conspiracy. "The young rascal must have stolen the powder to be used for blasting. Well, his father can pay the damages, as he has done a hundred times before; and I suppose it will be all right then."

We went into the engine-room, and took seats with Christy Holgate, who manifested no little interest in the affair of the morning.

"The little villain intends to have you mixed up

in the scrape somehow, Wolf," continued my father, who could not turn his attention from the subject.

"I don't care if he does. I didn't do anything, and I'm willing to face the music," I replied, confidently. "I took his pistol away from him to keep him from shooting me; but I mean to give it back to him as soon as we return."

"I hope it will be all right, Wolf," said my father, anxiously.

"Your boy ain't to blame, Ralph," added Christy, the engineer.

"I know he isn't; but Colonel Wimpleton is the worst man to get along with in the world when Waddie gets into a scrape with other boys. He thinks the little villain is an angel, and if he ever does any mischief he is led away by bad boys. Well, no matter; I am glad this thing takes place to-day instead of last week."

"Why so, father?" I asked.

"Don't you know what I am going up to Ucayga for, this morning?"

"No, sir; I haven't heard."

"Well, I talked it over long enough with **your** mother this morning."

" I wasn't there."

" I'll tell you, Wolf," replied my father, throwing one leg over the other, and looking particularly well satisfied with himself and all the rest of mankind. " When we first went to Centreport, I bought the place we live on of Colonel Wimpleton. I gave him one thousand down, and a note, secured by mortgage, for two thousand more. I think the place, to-day, is worth four thousand dollars."

" All of that," added Christy.

" Well, I've been saving up all my spare money ever since to pay off that mortgage, which expires next week. I have got the whole amount, and four hundred dollars more, in the bank at Ucayga, and I'm going to take it out to-day, and pay up. That's what's the matter, Wolf; but I don't quite like this row with Waddie."

Christy listened with quite as much interest as I did to the story of my father.

CHAPTER IV.

ON THE LOCOMOTIVE.

AFTER we had sufficiently discussed the explosion and my father's financial affairs, Christy Holgate took from under the seat where he sat a curiously-shaped black bottle and a tumbler. I would rather have seen him take a living rattlesnake from the box, and place it at my feet — or rather at my father's feet, for it was on his account that I shuddered when I heard the owner of the bottle declare that it contained "old rye whiskey." Christy told a tedious story about the contents of this "vial of wrath" — where it was distilled in the State of Kentucky; how a particular friend of his had procured two quarts of it, and no more of that year's manufacture could be had in the whole nation, either for love or for money.

One would have supposed, from the eloquent description of its virtues, that it was the nectar of the gods, instead of the fiery fluid which men put into their mouths to take their brains away. I was disgusted with the description, and I shuddered the more when I saw that my father was interested in it, and that he cast longing glances at the queer-shaped bottle. I had heard that my father lost his situation at the town on the Hudson by drinking to excess, and I trembled lest the old appetite should be revived in him. If he had been a man like Christy Holgate I should not have trembled, as I viewed the case, for he had drank liquor all his lifetime to moderation, and no one had ever known him to be intoxicated. It was not so with my father. He had struggled manfully against the insidious appetite, and, with only a couple of exceptions, he had always done so successfully. Twice, and twice only, had he been under the influence of liquor since he came to Centreport. I feared, if he tasted the contents of the strange-looking bottle, that the third time would have to be added to the list.

Christy poured out a glass of the " old rye " and my father drank it. The engineer of the boat took

one himself; and both of them talked very fast then
till the steamer arrived at her destination. I was
alarmed for my father's safety, and I tried to induce
him to go on shore the moment we reached the
wharf; but before we could leave Christy produced
the bottle again, and both of them took a second
dram, though I noticed that the engineer took a
very light one himself.

The effect upon my father was soon apparent,
though he did not appear to be actually intoxicated.
He did not stagger, but he talked in a loud and
reckless manner. He gave me a dollar, and told me
to spend it for anything I wanted. He said it was
a holiday, and he wished me to have a good time.
I put the dollar in my pocket, but I did not leave
my father. I was mortified by his blustering speech
and extravagant manner, but I still clung to him.
I hoped my presence would prevent him from taking another dram; and I think it did; for though,
on our way to the bank, we passed several bar-
rooms, he did not offer to enter one of them. Two
or three times he hinted to me that I had better
go and enjoy myself alone, which assured me that

he desired to drink again, but did not wish to do so before me.

I have since learned that a man will always, be more circumspect before his children than when away from them. He feels his responsibility at such times, and is unwilling to degrade himself before those who are his natural dependents. I told my father I had no place to go to, that I did not wish to buy anything, and that I preferred to remain with him. He was vexed at my obstinacy, but he did not say anything. We went to the bank together, and he drew out his money, twenty-four hundred dollars — more than he had ever possessed at one time before. It would discharge the mortgage on the place, and leave him four hundred dollars to make certain improvements which he contemplated.

The whiskey which he had drank made him feel rich, and it pained me to see him manifest his feelings in a very ridiculous way. He put the money in a great leather pocket-book he carried, and placed it in his breast pocket. By various little devices I induced him to return to the steamer with me.

When it was too late I was sorry I had done so, for Christy Holgate again placed the bottle to his lips taking hardly a teaspoonful of its contents himself. It would be an hour before the train arrived, whose passengers the steamer was to convey up the lake, and I trembled for the safety of my father and of the large sum of money he had in his pocket.

It seems very strange to me, and I dare say it has seemed so to others, that some men, when they have the greatest work of their lifetime in hand, or are pressed down by the heaviest responsibility that ever weighed upon them, choose this very time to get intoxicated. My father had certainly done so. With more than two thirds of his worldly wealth in his pocket, he had taken to drinking whiskey — a thing he had not done before for at least a year. Half of the hour we had to wait had passed away, and my poor father made himself very ridiculous. I had never felt so bad before in my life.

"Wolf, my boy, I forgot to get my tobacco when I was up in town," said he, handing me a quarter.

"Run up to that store next to the hotel, and get me half a pound of his best plug."

I did not want to leave him, but I could not disobey without making a terrible scene. I went as fast as my legs would carry me, and returned out of breath with running. My father had drank nothing during my absence, and I was startled when I beheld his changed appearance on my return. He was deadly pale, and was trembling with emotion. He was searching his pockets, and gazing nervously into every hole and corner in the engine-room, where I found him.

"What is the matter, father?" I asked, alarmed at his appearance.

"I have lost my pocket-book, Wolf," gasped he, in an awful and impressive whisper.

"Lost it!" I exclaimed, almost paralyzed by the intelligence.

"Nonsense, Ralph!" added Christy, with a forced laugh. "You can't have lost it, if you had it when you came here."

"I did have it; I know I did. I felt it in my pocket after I came on board."

"Then it must be in your pocket now. You haven't been out of the engine-room since you came," persisted Christy.

I helped my father search his pockets; but the pocket-book was certainly gone.

"You must have dropped it out on your way down from the bank," said the engineer.

"How could I drop it out?" groaned my father, as he pointed to the deep pocket in which he always kept it.

I searched again in every part of my father's clothing, but in vain. He was perfectly sober now, so far as I could judge, the grief and mortification attending his heavy loss having neutralized the effects of the liquor. On the seat stood the queer-shaped bottle from which my father had imbibed confusion. By its side was the tumbler, half filled with the whiskey. I concluded that it had been poured out for my father, and that the discovery of his loss had prevented him from drinking it. I put them on the floor and looked into the box; I examined every part of the engine-room again, but without success. The missing treasure could not be found.

My father sat down upon the box again, and actually wept for grief and shame. I heard the whistle of the approaching train. It seemed to startle the victim of the whiskey bottle from his sad revery. He removed his hands from his face, and glanced at Christy, with a look which was full of meaning to me, and seemed to be quite intelligible to the engineer.

"I guess I'll take a look on the wharf," said Christy, beginning to edge slowly out of the engine-room.

"Christy Holgate," cried my father, springing at the throat of the engineer, and clutching him like a madman, "you have got my money!"

"Why, Ralph, what ails you? Do you think I'd take your money?" replied Christy; but his face was as pale as my father's and his lip quivered.

"I know you have! That's what you made me drunk for," continued my father savagely, as he began to claw into the garments of the engineer, in seach of his treasure.

Christy started as though he had been stung by a serpent when my father placed his hand upon his

4

breast pocket, and a violent struggle ensued. As my maddened parent tore open his coat, I distinctly saw enough of the well-known pocket-book to enable me to identify it. He had taken it from my father's pocket and transferred it to his own while handing him the glass of whiskey.

"He has it, father!" I shouted. "I see it in his pocket."

Christy was a powerful man, and with a desperate effort he shook off my father, hurling him upon the floor with much violence. Having shaken off his fierce assailant, he rushed from the engine-room to the gang-plank forward, by which the passengers were coming on board, and disappeared in the crowd. Without waiting to learn the condition of my father, I followed him. I lost sight of him in the throng, but I commenced an earnest search for him. Presently I discovered him skulking along by the train on the side opposite that at which the passengers were getting out.

The engine had been detached from the train, and had moved forward to the water tank to have her tender filled. The engineer had left the locomotive to speak with a friend on the wharf; and the fireman, after the tender was filled, helped the men throw in the wood. I went ahead of the engine, where I could observe the movements of Christy. I thought he would hide till the train started, and then jump on board. If he did, I meant to be a passenger on the same train.

The tender was filled with wood, and the men walked away, including the fireman. The moment they had gone, Christy sneaked along by the wood-sheds, and jumped upon the locomotive. He could not see me, for I was concealed by the smoke-stack. He started the engine. I jumped upon the cow-catcher. In a moment, as he let on the steam, the locomotive was flying like lightning over the rails. I clung to the cow-catcher till the motion was steady, and then climbed up to the side of the machine, exhibiting myself to the astonished villain. At this moment, I happened to think of Waddie's revolver in my pocket. It was a useful plaything for an emergency like this, and I drew it forth.

CHAPTER V.

CHRISTY HOLGATE.

"STOP her!" I shouted again and again to Christy Holgate, as I pointed the pistol at his head through the window of the cab.

When I first made my appearance, he had thrust his head and shoulders through the window, apparently to examine the situation, and determine in what manner he could best dispose of me. I threatened to shoot him, and he drew in his head, placing himself where I could not see him without changing my position.

I pointed the pistol at Christy and threatened to fire; but I had as little taste for shooting a man as I had for eating him, and I beg the privilege of adding, that I am not a cannibal. I found it very easy to talk about firing, but very much harder to do it. Christy had proved that he was a villain,

and a very mean villain too; but I found it quite impossible to carry my threat into execution. I could reason it out that he deserved to be shot, and as he was running away with my father's money, and did not stop the engine when I told him to do so, that it would be perfectly right for me to shoot him.

If I had been a bloodthirsty, brutal monster, instead of an ordinary boy of sixteen, with human feelings, I suppose I could have fired the pistol while the muzzle covered the head of the rascal in the cab. If I had not been afraid of killing him, I think I should have fired; for I had considerable confidence in my skill as a marksman, though it had not been fortified by much practical experience.

Though Christy had been very useful in enabling me to enlarge my knowledge of the mysteries of the marine engine, and though I was reasonably grateful to him for the privilege he had afforded me, I did not feel under great obligations to him. Whenever I made a trip with him in the engine-room, for the purpose of studying my favorite theme, he invariably set me at work upon some dirty job, either at oiling the machinery or cleaning the bright parts. He was rather stout, and it was always my function to climb up and oil the gudgeons and other working parts of the walking-beam. I had done almost everything pertaining to an engine, under his direction. He used to praise me without stint, and call me a smart boy; which perhaps he intended as my reward, though I found it in the knowledge and experience I had gained.

I did not refrain from pressing the trigger of the revolver while aiming it at Christy's head on account of the debt of obligation which weighed me down. I knew enough about an engine to make myself useful, and I worked hard for all the information I obtained. Still I considered myself indebted to him for the opportunities he had afforded me; and, if he had not chosen to be a villain, I am quite sure I should always have felt grateful to him, even while I paid in hard work for every scrap of knowledge I obtained from him.

Christy and my father were quite intimate; though, as the steamer in which he served always lay nights and Sundays at the lower end of the lake, they had

not been together much of late years. He had rec-
ommended my father for the position he then held
in the flour mills. I know that my father felt under
great obligations to him for the kind words he had
spoken in his favor, and had often urged me to help
him all I could, encouraging me by the hope that
I might, by and by, get a place as engineer on a
steamboat.

The engineer of the Ruoara — for this was the
name of the steamer in which we had gone down
to Ucayga — was a strange man in some respects.
He made a great deal of the service he had rendered to my father and to me, and very little of the
service we had rendered to him, for my father had
often made him little presents, often lent him money,
and had once, when the mills were not working, run
his steamer for him a week, while he was sick, without any compensation. I never thought Christy had
any cause to complain of either of us. But I dislike
this balancing of mutual obligations, and only do it
in self-defence; for it is the kindness of the heart,
and the real willingness to do another a favor, which
constitute the obligation, rather than what is actually

done. "And if ye do good to them that do good
to you, what thank have ye ? For sinners also do
even the same."

Christy was a man who always believed that the
world was using him hardly. He was unlucky, in
his own estimation. The world never gave him his
due, and everybody seemed to get the better of him.
Though he had good wages, he was not worth any
money. He spent his earnings as fast as he got
them; not in dissipation, that I am aware of, but
he had a thriftless way of doing business. He never
could get rid of the suspicion that the world in gen-
eral was cheating him; and for this reason he had
an old grudge against the world. On the passage to
Ucayga he discoursed in his favorite strain with my
father when he learned his errand. The unhappy
man seemed to think that it was unjust to him for
one in the same calling to have twenty-four hundred dollars in cash, while he had not a dollar
beyond his wages.

The engineer of the steamer had not pluck enough
to resent and resist injustice. Perhaps he thought
that, in introducing my father to his situation, he

had been the making of him, and that he was therefore entitled to the lion's share of his savings for
five years. Whatever he thought, he had deliber-
ately formed his plan to rob my father of his money,
and had actually succeeded in his purpose. Christy
knew the weak point of his intended victim, and
had plied him with whiskey till he was in a situation to be operated upon with impunity. I think
my father wanted to drink again, and had sent me
for the tobacco so that I should not see him do so.

My father afterwards told me that he recalled the
movements of Christy when he took the pocket-book
from him, though he thought nothing of them at
the time.

"Ralph, you are a good fellow — the best fellow
out! Let's take one more drink," said Christy, as
reported by my father.

"I'm a good fellow, Christy, and you're another,"
replied the victim. "Just one more drink;" and my
father, in his maudlin affection for his friend, had
thrown his arms around his neck, and hugged him.

During this inebriated embrace Christy had taken
the money from his pocket. After he had poured

out the liquor, he found that his pocket-book was gone. The discovery paralyzed him; but his head was too much muddled at first to permit him to reason on the circumstances. He remembered that he had felt the pocket-book only a few minutes before; and, as soon as he could think, he was satisfied that his companion had robbed him, for the simple reason that no one else had been near him. He was ashamed of his own conduct. He was conscious that he had drank too much, and that this had been the occasion of his misfortune.

I do not know what Christy's plan was, or how he expected to escape the consequences of his crime. He had easily shaken my father off, and made his escape. However hardly the world had used him, he was certainly more severe upon himself than his tyrant had ever been; for when a man commits a crime, he treats himself worse than any other man can treat him. I could not fathom the villain's plan in running away with the locomotive. I doubt whether he had any purpose except to escape from immediate peril, and thus secure his ill-gotten prize.

The circumstances had devolved upon me the responsibility of capturing the treacherous friend. Half a dozen times I threatened to shoot him if he did not stop the engine, but somehow my muscles did not seem to have the power to execute the threat. Christy had placed himself where I could not see him through the cab window. I examined the revolver, which contained two charges, and then walked up to the window. The villain had crouched down by the fire-box, evidently having a wholesome regard for the weapon in my hand. The engine was going at the rate of thirty miles an hour, and I judged that we had gone about ten miles.

" Christy Holgate, I don't want to shoot you, but I'll do it, as sure as you live, if you don't stop her ! " I shouted, as loud as I could yell, while I aimed the revolver at him again.

" Don't fire, Wolf, and I'll stop her as soon as I can," he replied; and I think his guilty conscience terrified him quite as much as the pistol.

He stood up, and I saw the pocket-book sticking out of his outside breast pocket. I concluded that he had taken it out to examine its contents, and I

felt pretty confident that I should have the satisfaction of restoring the lost treasure to my father.
With the revolver, containing two bullets, I realized
that I was master of the situation.

Christy shut off the steam, and put on the brake
just as we entered a dense wood. As the speed of
the engine slackened, I climbed upon the roof of
the cab, and jumped down upon the wood in the
tender. I took care not to go very near the villain,
for, even with the pistol in my hand, I thought he
was fully a match for me.

"Do you mean to shoot me, after all I've done
for you, Wolf?" said he, in a whining tone, as the
engine stopped.

"I didn't think you would serve my father such a
mean trick as you did," I replied. "I will shoot
you if you don't give up that pocket-book."

"I didn't mean to take your father's money, Wolf.
He and I have been good friends for a great many
years, and I wouldn't hurt him any more than I
would myself."

"But you did take it."

"I didn't mean to keep it. I was only joking. I

meant to give it back to him; but when he flew at me so, he made me mad."

"What did you run away on the engine for, then?" I demanded, willing, if possible, to accept his explanation.

"You got me into the scrape, and I hardly knew what I was about. I'm ruined now, and it won't do for me to go back."

"You can go where you please; but give me that pocket-book, Christy, or we'll finish the business here," I continued, raising the pistol again.

"Of course I'll give it to you," he answered, handing me the pocket-book. "But I'm afraid to go back myself."

I put the treasure into my pocket, and felt that I had won the day. Christy jumped from the engine, and disappeared in the woods.

CHAPTER VI.

ON THE LOCOMOTIVE.

I WAS entirely satisfied with myself as I put the pocket-book into my breast pocket, and carefully buttoned my coat. I felt as though I had really done "a big thing," allowing the phrase to mean even more than boys usually attach to it. How my father would rejoice to see that money again! How thankful he would be for the success which had attended my efforts!

The pocket-book was in my possession, and I was too much excited to look into it. I was somewhat afraid, if I did not keep both eyes open, that Christy would come out of the woods and undo the work I had accomplished. I could hear him forcing his way through the underbrush as he retreated; but I still kept the revolver where I could make use of it if occasion required. It seemed to me then that my quarrel with Mr. Waddie had been a fortunate circumstance, since the possession of the pistol had enabled me to recover the pocket-book. I was rather thankful to the scion for his agency in the matter, and willing, when the time of settlement came, to make some concessions, if needful, to his vanity and pride.

Christy had piled the wood into the fire-box for a hard run, and the locomotive was hissing and quivering with the pressure of steam upon it. By the unwritten law of succession, the care of the machine devolved upon me, and I am willing to confess that I was not displeased with the task imposed upon me. To run the engine alone, with no one to volunteer any instructions or limitations to me, was a delightful duty; and I was so absorbed by the prospect that I gave no further thought to the pocket-book. It was safe, and that was enough.

I must run the locomotive back to Ucayga; but I was fully equal to the task. I knew every part of the machine, and had entire confidence in my own ability. I did not exactly like to run her backwards; but, as there was no turn-table at hand, I had no choice. Reversing the valves, I let on the steam very gradually, and the engine moved off according to my calculations. I gave her more steam, and she began to rush over the rails at a velocity which startled me, when I considered that the motions of the machine were under my control.

I had to keep a lookout over the top of the tender, and at the same time watch the furnace, the gauge-cocks, and the indicator; and of course I had to observe them much more closely than would have been necessary for a person of more experience. Having my hands and my head full, something less than thirty miles an hour was sufficient to gratify my ambition. I knew nothing about the roads which crossed the track, and therefore I kept up a constant whistling and ringing of the bell. It was exciting, I can testify, to any one who never tried to run a locomotive under similar circumstances. I was doing duty as engineer and fireman, and I could not think of anything but the business in hand.

It would have been exceedingly awkward and unpleasant to burst the boiler, or run over a vehicle crossing the track, and I did not wish to have my first venture on a locomotive damaged by such an accident. I kept a sharp lookout, both before and behind me. It was a new position to me, and I enjoyed the novelty of it, in spite of the fear of being blown up, or smashed by a collision. I kept the whistle sounding, and as the engine whirled around a bend, after I had been running fifteen or twenty minutes, I saw some men lifting a hand-car from the track in great haste. They had heard my warning in season to prevent the catastrophe I dreaded.

"Stop her!" shouted one of the party, with all his might, as the engine thundered by him.

A glance at the party assured me that one of them was the engineer of the train. I shut off the steam, and put on the brake. As it was a down grade, the engine went about a mile before I could stop her. But, as soon as I had brought her to a halt, I reversed the valves again, and went ahead till I came up with the party, who were just putting the hand-car upon the track again. The engineer and fire-man leaped upon the foot-board. The former was much excited, and I was not a little surprised to

5

find that he did not even thank me for bringing back his engine.

"What does all this mean?" he demanded, with an oath. "What did you run away with the engine for?"

"I did not run away with her; I only brought her back," I replied, indignantly.

"Who was the man that stole the money?"

"That was Christy Holgate; he was the man that ran away with the engine."

"Who are you?"

"I'm Wolf Penniman. The money was stolen from my father. When I saw Christy leap into the cab, I jumped upon the cow-catcher."

"Then you are the boy they were looking for down to the station."

"I don't know about that. I had a pistol, and I made Christy stop her, and give me the pocket-book. He got off then, and ran into the woods. I ran the engine back again."

"I'm sorry you didn't shoot the rascal," added the engineer, as he examined into the condition of the locomotive.

"I got the pocket-book again, and that was all I wanted. I didn't wish to kill him."

"Who told you how to run an engine?" asked the engineer, as he started the locomotive.

"My father is an engineer, and I've always been among engines, though I never ran a locomotive alone before."

"I suppose you think you can run one now?"

"Yes, sir; I can put her through by daylight," I replied, using a pet phrase of mine.

"You have done very well, sonny," said he, with a smile; and he could afford to smile, though he growled a great deal at being an hour behind time by the event of losing his engine.

He asked me a great many questions about Christy and the robbery; and the conversation was only interrupted by our arrival at the Ucayga station, where the impatient passengers were waiting to continue their journey. I jumped off; the engine was shackled to the train again, and went on its way.

"Halloo, Wolf!" called the captain of the steamer to me. "Where is Christy?"

"I don't know, sir. He jumped off the locomotive, and ran away into the woods."

A crowd of people gathered around me to hear my story, for the facts of the robbery had been related by my father. I felt the pocket-book in my coat, and declined to answer any questions till I had seen my father. I was told he was on board of the steamer, and I hastened to find him. He was in the engine-room, where I had left him. He was still deadly pale, and seemed to have grown ten years older in a single hour.

"Where have you been, Wolf?" asked he, in a voice almost choking with emotion.

"I have been after Christy."

"Did you catch him?" he asked, in a sepulchral tone.

"I was on the engine with him. Here is your pocket-book, father."

He grasped it with convulsive energy, and seemed to grow young again in a moment. The crowd, most of whom were passengers in the steamer, gathered in the gangway, by the side of the engine-room, to learn the facts. In an excited manner I began to tell my story.

"What does he say? Speak louder, boy!" called the men behind me.

Though I did not feel like haranguing a multitude, I raised my voice.

"Good! Good!" shouted the crowd, when I came to the point where I aimed the revolver at Christy in the cab. "Why didn't you shoot him?"

"When I drew a bead upon him he stopped the engine, and gave up the pocket-book," I continued, with boyish exhilaration.

"Wolf, you have saved me," gasped my delighted father; "but I am rather sorry you did not shoot the villain."

"We are wasting the whole day here," said the captain of the boat, nervously. "We have no engineer now. Ralph, will you run us up the lake?"

"Certainly I will," replied my father, taking his place at the machinery.

I sat down in the engine-room with him and answered the questions he put to me about the affair. He obeyed the signals given him by the bells, and as soon as the boat was going ahead at full speed, he took a seat at my side.

"Wolf, I have suffered more to-day than in all the rest of my lifetime," said he, wiping the perspiration from his brow. "If I had lost that money, it would well nigh have killed me. It was a lucky thing that you took that pistol from Waddie."

"It happened just right; Christy was afraid of it, and when I got the muzzle to bear upon him, he came down, like Crockett's coon," I answered, with no little self-complaisance.

"Was he willing to give it up?"

"He couldn't help himself. If he hadn't given it up, I should have put a bullet through him."

"I'm glad you didn't have to do that; on the whole, though, I shouldn't have cared much if you had shot him," added my father, putting his hand upon the pocket-book to assure himself of its present safety. "I wouldn't have believed Christy could be guilty of such a mean trick. But it was my fault, Wolf. You saw how it was done, and it has been a lesson to me which I shall never forget."

My father sighed heavily as he thought of the circumstances, and I fancy he promised himself then never again to touch whiskey.

"Did Christy open the pocket-book?" he asked, after a silence of some minutes.

" I don't know. I didn't see him open it, and I don't know when he could have had time to do so," I replied.

" It don't look as though it had been touched," said he, taking the pocket-book from his pocket, and proceeding to open it.

" I guess it is all right, father," I added.

" All right!" gasped he. " There is not a single dollar in it!"

My father groaned in bitterness of spirit. I looked into the open pocket-book. The money had all been taken from it!

CHAPTER VII.

THE VIAL OF WRATH.

I WAS both amazed and confounded when it was ascertained that the pocket-book did not contain the money. From the depth of despair my father and myself had gone up to the pinnacle of hope, when the treasure was supposed to be found; and now we fell back into a deeper gulf than that into which we had first fallen. Those with whom money is plenty cannot understand the greatness of my father's loss. For years he had toiled and saved in order to clear the house in which we lived. He had struggled with, and conquered, the appetite for intoxicating drinks, in order to accomplish his great purpose.

He had been successful. He had kept away from the drunkard's bowl, he had lived prudently, he had carefully husbanded all his resources, .and, at the time my story begins, he felt that the pretty little place where we lived actually belonged to him. It was always to be the home of his family, and it was all the more loved and prized because it had been won by constant toil and careful saving. This was the feeling of my father, as it was my own, when we started for Ucayga to draw the money from the bank. We felt like the king and the prince who had won a great victory, and were to march in triumph into the conquered possession.

My father was elated by what he had accomplished. The mortgage note for two thousand dollars would be due the next week, and he had the money to pay it, with enough to make the coveted improvements. It would have been better if he had not been elated; for this feeling led him to believe that, as the battle had been won, there was no longer any need of the vigilance with which he had guarded himself. He had raised the cup to his lips, and in a moment, as it were, his brilliant fortune deserted him; the savings of years were wrenched from his relaxed grasp.

I do not wonder, as I consider how prudent and

careful he had been, that he sank into the depths of despair when he found the money was really gone. The struggle had been long and severe, the victory sublime and precious; and now the defeat, in the moment of conquest, was terrible in the extreme. I trembled for my father while I gazed into his pale face, and observed the sweep of his torturing emotions, as they were displayed in his expression.

For my own part, I was intensely mortified at the result of my efforts. I felt cheap and mean, as I sank down from the height to which I had lifted myself, and realized that all my grand deeds had been but a farce. If I had only looked into the pocket-book when Christy returned it to me, I might have saved this terrible fall. The villain had probably taken the money from it while he was crouching down by the fire-box. He had played a trick upon me, and I had been an easy victim. I was but a boy, while I had felt myself to be a man, and had behaved like a boy. If I had been smart in one respect, I had been stupid in another. I blamed myself severely for permitting myself to be duped by Christy at the moment when he was in my power. I almost wished that I had shot him; but I am sure now that I should have felt ten times worse if I had killed him, even if I had obtained the money by doing so.

"I am ruined, Wolf," groaned my father, as he dropped upon the seat in the engine-room. "I shall never get the money now."

"I think you will, father," I replied, trying to be hopeful rather than confident.

"No; I shall never see a dollar of it again."

"Don't give it up yet, father. Christy has gone off in his every-day clothes, and left his family at Ucayga. He will come back again, or you will get some clew to him."

"I'm afraid not," said my father, shaking his head.

"But something must be done. Christy isn't a great way off, and we must put him through by daylight," I added.

"What can we do? It isn't much use to do any thing."

"Yes, it is. Something can be done, I know."

"Where are we now, Wolf?" asked my father.

I did not know where we were, for there was no chance to see the shore from the engine-room. I walked out on the forward deck, and returned immediately.

"Well, where are we, Wolf?" demanded my father, rather sharply, as he laid down the glass from which he had just drained another dram taken from Christy's queer-shaped bottle.

"We are just off the North Shoe," I replied, as gloomily as though another third of my father's worldly wealth had also taken to itself wings.

My poor father was drinking whiskey again. In his depression and despair, the bottle seemed to be his only resource. I have since learned enough of human nature to understand how it was with him. Men in the sunlight of prosperity play with the fiend of the cup. Full of life, full of animal spirits, it is comparatively easy to control the appetite. But when the hour of despondency comes; when depression invades the mind; when earthly possessions elude the grasp — then they flee to the consolations of the cup. It gives an artificial strength, and men who in prosperity might always have kept sober and temperate, in adversity are lost in the whirlpool of tippling and inebriation.

Thus it seemed to be with my father. He had begun to drink that day in the elation of his spirits; he was now resorting to the cup as an antidote for depression and despair. The dram had its temporary effect; but, while he was cheered by the fiery draught, I trembled for him. I feared that this was only the beginning of the end — that he needed prosperity to save him from himself.

"Off the North Shoe," said he; but he was not ably wholly to conceal his vexation that I had seen him take the glass from his lips. "We shall be in Ruoara in half an hour, and I will send a sheriff after the villain. You say Christy went about ten miles, Wolf?"

"Yes, sir; as nearly as I could guess."

"We'll catch him yet," added my father, confidently. "Have an eye to the engine, Wolf, while I go and see the captain about it."

My father left the engine-room, which he would not have done if he had not supposed me entirely competent to run the machine. I determined to have an eye to something besides the engine. In my father's present state of mind, I feared he would drink till he was helpless. I raised the lid of the seat and took out the strange bottle. It was about half full. There was mischief enough left in it to rob my father of all his senses.

Even as a boy I prided myself on my promptness in action. The present seemed to be a moment when it was my duty to cast out an evil spirit. I took the bottle to the gangway, where there was a large scupper-hole to let the water run off when the decks were washed down. Into this I emptied the contents of the "vial of wrath." The fiery liquid ran through and mingled with the clear waters of the lake. Having no spite against the bottle, I returned it to the locker in the engine-room, rather to save my father the trouble of looking for it than because I had any regard for its preservation.

Presently my father returned with the captain of the steamer, who did not seem to relish the idea of leaving the engine in charge of a boy of fifteen. They talked about the lost money, and my father was tolerably cheerful under the influence of the dram he had taken. The captain said that Mr. Mortimer, the sheriff, was almost always on the wharf when the steamer made her landing, and that he would be glad to start instantly in pursuit of the robber. It was a kind of business which he enjoyed, and if any one could catch Christy, he could. I was quite satisfied with this arrangement, and so was my father.

When the boat touched at Ruoara, Mr. Mortimer was on the pier, as the captain had said he would be. He was more than willing to undertake the task of pursuing the thief, and the steamer was detained at the landing long enough for him to procure a warrant for the arrest of the fugitive. He was to cross the lake to the next port on the other side, from which he was to proceed, by private conveyance, to the town nearest to the point where Christy had left the locomotive. Mr. Mortimer came into the engine-room as the boat started, and we gave him all the information we possessed in regard to the robber.

"Now, Mortimer, won't you take something before you go ashore?" said my father.

"Thank you, I don't care if I do," replied the sheriff. "I have had a cold for two or three days and a little of the ardent won't hurt me, though I am not in the habit of taking it very often."

"It will do you good; it does me good," added my father, as he raised the lid of the locker and took out the queer bottle.

The "vial of wrath" was empty. My father looked at me — looked uglier than I had ever seen him look before. He held it over the glass, and inverted it. My work had been thoroughly accomplished, and hardly a drop of the fiery fluid answered the summons to appear. My father looked at me again. His lips were compressed, and his eyes snapped with anger.

"All gone — is it?" laughed the sheriff. "Well, no matter; I can get along without it."

"We'll take some at the bar," said my father, as the bell rang to "slow" her.

When the boat was fast to the wharf, they went

to the bar and drank together. Somehow, it seemed to me that all my calculations were failing on that day; but still I hoped to accomplish something by the deed I had done. Mr. Mortimer went on shore, and my father returned to the engine-room. I hoped he would be satisfied with the dram he had taken, and that I should escape the consequences of his anger. The bell rang, and the boat started again.

"Wolf, did you empty that bottle?" asked my father, sternly.

"Yes, sir, I did," I replied, gently, but firmly.

"What did you do that for?"

"I thought it was best not to have the liquor here," I answered, with no little trepidation.

"Best!" exclaimed he. "Who made you a keeper over me?"

I did not dare to say anything. I held my peace, resolved to endure the storm in silence, lest some disrespectful word should escape my lips. My father was very angry, and I feared that, under the influence of the liquor, he would do violence to me; but he did not.

"Get away from here! Don't let me see you around me any longer," said he, at last, when he found that I was not disposed to explain my conduct, or to cast any reproaches upon him.

I went to the forward deck, and seated myself on the rail at the bow.

CHAPTER VIII.

THE DUMMY ENGINE.

MY father and I had always been on the best of terms. He was very considerate to me, and used to talk with me a great deal; indeed, he treated me in such a way that I had very little reason to think I was a boy. He discussed his plans with me, and often asked my advice, just as though I had been a man of mature judgment. He was angry with me now, almost for the first time in my remembrance; certainly he had never before been so highly exasperated with me. But I consoled myself with the reflection that he was partially intoxicated, and that, when the fumes of the whiskey had worked off, he would be as kind and gentle to me as ever.

Perhaps it was wrong for me to empty the bottle; but, as I can never know what would have happened if I had not done so, I am content with simply believing that I did it for the best. He was in charge of the engine. There were fifty precious lives on the boat. My father had the reputation of being a very steady and reliable man. If he had been a little noisy and turbulent at Ucayga, the shock of losing his money had wrought a sudden and wonderful change in his manner, so that few, if any, had noticed him. After the steamer started, I alone was aware of his condition; I alone knew of his resuming his cups; and I alone knew that, left to himself, he would soon be intoxicated, and incapable of managing the engine. I could not wish that I had not emptied the bottle, even while I suffered intensely under the consciousness of his displeasure.

While I was thinking of the wrath of my father, and of the consequences which might follow the loss of the money, the steamer approached Middle-port, which was opposite Centreport, where we lived. My attention was immediately attracted by a singular-looking object on the canal boat at the wharf. My thoughts were partially diverted for a time from the painful circumstances of our family affairs, and I gazed with interest at the strange object. It looked like an immense omnibus, only it had a smoke-stack passing through the roof at one end. I had never seen such a thing before, and I did not know what to make of it.

"Ah, the dummy has arrived," said a Middleport passenger, who had come forward to look at the carriage.

"The what, sir?" I asked.

"The dummy."

"What's a dummy?" I inquired; for, with all my study of steam-engines, I had never heard of one.

"It's a railroad car with an engine in one end of it," replied the gentleman; and by this time I could make out the form of the thing. "It is for the Lake Shore Railroad. I suppose you have heard that the students of the Toppleton Institute are building a railroad on the shore of the lake."

"Yes, sir, I have heard of it."

"This dummy was built to run on a horse rail-road in Philadelphia; but though they call it a dummy, it made so much noise, and frightened so many horses, they could not use it in the streets. Major Toppleton saw it, and bought it cheap, for the students, in order to get a little ahead of the Wimpleton Institute, on the other side of the lake."

As the boat approached the wharf, I examined the dummy very carefully. It was a railway carriage, similar to those used on street roads, having an engine in one end to propel it. It would be a rare plaything for the Toppletonians, and I envied them the possession of such a prize. I knew all about the Lake Shore Railroad, and many a pang of jealousy had it caused the Wimpletonians, on our side of the lake; for a stupendous rivalry existed between the two Institutes, which were separated from each other by only a mile of fresh water.

Lake Ucayga is about forty-five miles long. At the foot of it was the town of the same name, connected with the great centres of travel by railroad. At the head of the lake was the large town of Hitaca. The average width of the lake was three miles; but near the middle — or, to be more accurate, twenty miles from Ucayga, and twenty-five from Hitaca — a point of land jutted out on the west side, so as to leave a passage only a mile in width. On this peninsula was located the town of Middleport, and directly opposite was Centreport.

Below these towns the country was level, while above them it was hilly, and even mountainous near the head of the lake. Middleport and Centreport were of very modern origin, so far as their social and commercial importance was concerned, and their growth and history were somewhat remarkable. They are located on the verge of the hilly region, and the scenery around them, without being grand or sublime, is very beautiful.

Hardly twenty years before my story opens, two gentlemen had come up to the lake to spend a week in hunting and fishing. They were fast friends, and each of them had made an immense fortune in the China trade. The narrow part of the lake — generally called "The Narrows" — attracted their attention on account of its picturesque scenery. They were delighted with the spot, and the result was, that, on retiring from business, they fixed their residences here.

One of these gentlemen was Colonel Wimpleton, and the other was Major Toppleton. They had won their military titles in the same regiment of militia in their earlier life, and had clung together like brothers for many years. They built their elegant mansions on the banks of the lake, facing each other, and formerly gayly-painted barges were continually plying between them. Certainly their houses looked like palaces of enchantment, so elegantly were the grounds laid out, and so picturesque were the surroundings. In front of each, on the lake, was a wall of dressed stone, from the quarries in the neighborhood. From these walls, the grounds, covered with the richest green in summer, sloped gradually up to the houses. They were adorned with smooth walks and avenues, shaded with a variety of trees. Indeed, I think nothing more lovely was ever seen or imagined.

Major Toppleton, on the Middleport side, built a flour mill; the village began to grow, and soon became a place of considerable commercial importance. At the same time, Centreport increased in population and wealth, though not so rapidly as its neighbor on the other side of the lake. Both the gentlemen had sons; and they were alive to the importance of giving them a good education. This consideration induced them to discuss the propriety of establishing an academy, and both agreed that such an institution was desirable, especially as there was not one of high standing within fifty miles of the place. Then the difficult and delicate question of the location of the proposed academy came up for settlement. Each of them wanted it on his side of the lake; and on this rock the two friends, who had been almost brothers for forty years, split; and the warmth of their former friendship seemed to be the gauge of their present enmity.

The feud waxed fierce and bitter; and henceforth Middleport and Centreport, which had always been twin sisters, were savage foes. The major built a lofty edifice and called it the Toppleton Institute. The colonel, not to be thwarted or outdone, built another on a grander scale, and called it the Wimpleton Institute. Everything that could add to the efficiency and the popularity of the two institutions was liberally supplied; and, as competition is the life of trade, as well in literary as in commercial affairs, both thrived splendidly. All the principal cities and towns of the Union were represented among the students. The patron *millionnaire* of each, with his principal and teachers, labored and studied to devise some new schemes which would add to the popularity of his institution. Military drill, gymnastics, games, boating, English, French, and German systems were introduced, and dispensed with as fresher novelties were presented.

The rival academies numbered about a hundred students each, and neither seemed to obtain any permanent advantage over the other. " Like master like man;" and, as the major and the colonel quarrelled, the pupils could hardly help following their illustrious example; so that it was fortunate a mile of deep water lay between the two.

The rivalry of the *millionnaires* was not confined to the schools; it extended to the towns themselves. Colonel Wimpleton built a flour mill on the Centreport side, and fought boldly and cunningly for

the commercial salvation of his side of the lake. If
a bank, an insurance company, or a sawmill was
established in Middleport, another immediately appeared in Centreport; and the converse of the proposition was equally true.

In the midst of this rivalry the Toppleton Institute was vivified by a new idea. The mania for
building railroads which pervaded the Northern
States invaded the quiet haunts of learning. Many
of the students were the sons of prominent railroad
men, and Major Toppleton hit upon the magnificent
scheme of giving the young gentlemen a railroad
education. A company had been organized; certificates of stocks and bonds — of which the munificent
patron of the institution was the largest holder —
were issued. A president, directors, treasurer, and
clerk were elected; superintendents, track-masters,
baggage-masters, conductors, brakemen, engineers,
firemen, switch-tenders, and other officials were duly
appointed. At first the railroad was to be an imagi-
nary concern; but the wealthy patron was not content to have the business done on paper only. He
purchased sleepers and rails, and the students had

actually built five miles of road on the level border of the lake. The dummy engine had been
bought, and had been sent by railroad to the head
of the lake, and thence to Middleport by a canal
boat.

This splendid project of the Toppletonians was
viewed with consternation by the Wimpletonians.
I was warmly interested in the scheme, and watched
its progress with the deepest interest. The dummy
was a miracle to me, and I regarded it with the
most intense delight. All the Toppletonians, as-
sisted by a few men, were on the shore, busy as
bees in transferring the machine to the wharf.
Planks had been laid down on which to roll it
from the boat, and rigging manned by the students
was attached to it, by which it was to be hauled
on shore.

The steamer was to make a landing alongside
the canal boat. I stood at the bow watching the
operation of moving the dummy. They had rolled
it two or three feet up the skids; but "too many
cooks spoil the broth." A rope broke, the machine
slipped back, and, canting the boat by its impetus,

THE ACCIDENT TO THE DUMMY. — Page 93.

the thing rolled off, with a tremendous splash, into the lake. The steamer backed just in season to avoid smashing it into a hopeless wreck.

If Centreport had been there it would have rejoiced exceedingly at this mishap.

CHAPTER IX.

TOPPLETONIANS AND WIMPLETONIANS.

MIDDLEPORT had a terrible fall in the unfortunate slip of the dummy engine; and if any Wimpletonians, on the other side of the lake, witnessed the catastrophe, I am afraid they were ill-natured enough to "crow" over it; for to have seen the thing hissing up and down on the opposite shore would have been a sore trial to them. For the present, at least, it was safe on the bottom of the lake, though, as the water was only six or eight feet deep, the machine would doubtless be saved in the end.

Though I belonged to Centreport, and was a graduate of the Wimpleton Institute, I could not find it in my heart to rejoice at the disaster which had befallen the Toppletonians. I was too much interested in the dummy to cherish any ill-will towards the machine or its owners. I wanted to see it work, and I could not help envying the engineer who was to enjoy the superlative happiness of running it. Such a position would have suited me, and I was sorry the railroad idea had not originated on our side of the lake. I wondered what Colonel Wimpleton would bring forward to offset this novelty of his rival, not doubting that he would make a desperate effort to outdo the major.

The accident filled the Toppletonians with dismay. They had been yelling with excitement and delight while laboring at the skids and rigging; but now they were aghast and silent. The Ruoara backed away from the submerged machine, and made her landing at the end of the pier. The dummy rested upright upon the bottom of the lake, with its roof well out of the water. I hardly took my eyes off of it while we were at the wharf, and I only wished the task of putting it on the track of the Lake Shore Railroad had fallen on me; for I thought I saw a plan by which it could be easily accomplished.

While the steamer was waiting I stepped upon the wharf, and mingled with the crowd of dismayed

Toppletonians, who were gazing at the apparent wreck of all their hopes. I was acquainted with a few of them; but they regarded me with a feeling of jealousy and hatred which I am happy to state that I did not share with them.

"Our pipe is out," said Tommy Toppleton, the only son of the major. "It's too confounded bad! I meant to have a ride in that car by to-morrow."

"It's not so bad as it might be," I ventured to remark.

"Who are you?" snapped Tommy, when he recognized me as a Centreporter.

"I belong on the other side, I know; but I was really sorry to see the thing go overboard," I added, gently enough to disarm the wrath of the patron's son.

"I think the Wimpleton fellows will feel good over this," continued Tommy, who, if he had not been crestfallen at the misfortune of his clan, would have been impudent and overbearing to a plebeian like me.

"I suppose they will feel good; but if I were one of your fellows I would not let them enjoy it a great while. I would have it out of the water and get up steam before I slept upon it," I answered.

" What would you do?" asked Tommy curiously.

" I would get it out of the water in double-quick time, and then put her through by daylight, even if it took me all night."

" You are a brick, Wolf; and I am rather sorry you live on the other side of the lake," laughed the scion of the Middleport house. " Do you think you could get her out of the water?"

" I know I could."

" How would you do it?"

" I haven't time to explain it now," I replied, edging towards the steamer.

" I say, Wolf, people think you know all about an engine, and can run one as well as a man," continued Tommy, following me to the boat.

" I ran a locomotive ten miles to-day."

" Did you, though?"

" I did — all alone."

" Our fellows don't want a man for an engineer on the Lake Shore Railroad; some of them were talking about having you to run the dummy for us."

" I am much obliged to them for thinking of me."

" It's too bad you live on the other side."

I thought so too, as the bell of the Ruoara rang, and I stepped on board of her. To do anything for the enemy on the Middleport side would be to give mortal offence to Colonel Wimpleton, his hopeful son, and all the students of the Institute in Centreport; and it was quite out of the question for me to think of a position on the foot-board of the dummy. I would have given anything to join the Toppletonians, against whom I had now no spite, and take part in the operations of the new railroad; and I regarded it as a very great misfortune that the rivalry between the two places prevented me from doing so.

The Ruoara left the wharf, and stood across the lake towards Centreport. As she receded from the shore, I saw Tommy talking to his father, and pointing to the boat, as though I were the subject of the conversation. I do not know what either of them said; but the young gentleman doubtless told the patron of the Toppletonians that I considered myself able to extricate the dummy from her present position. I was a very modest young man at the time of which I write; but years have enabled me, in some measure, to conquer the feeling, and I may now say that I had a splendid reputation as an engineer, for a boy. I do not know that I was regarded as exactly a prodigy, but even men of ability treated me with great kindness and consideration on account of my proficiency in matters relating to machinery. It seemed quite possible, therefore, that Major Toppleton did not regard my suggestion of a plan to extricate the dummy as a mere boyish boast.

Whether he did or did not, I was too much oppressed by my father's misfortunes to think of the dummy after it was out of sight. I walked aft, passing through the gangway, where I could see my unfortunate parent. He looked stern and forbidding, and, when I paused at the door, he told me I need not stop there. I did not think he had been drinking again, and I felt sure that he would not long be angry. It made me very sad to think that he was offended with me; but, more than this, I dreaded lest he should fall back into his old habits, and become a drunkard.

As the steamer approached the Centreport landing, I was startled by three rousing cheers. On the lawn, which faced the river in front of the Wimpleton Institute, were assembled all the students. Two or three of them were looking through field glasses to the opposite shore. They had just discovered the nature of the disaster to the dummy, and they expressed their satisfaction in the cheers which I heard. It was mean and cowardly to rejoice in the misfortunes of others, even if they were enemies; but as their elders expressed themselves in this manner, nothing better could be expected of them.

I went ashore when the boat was made fast. I noticed that several people looked sharply at me, and some of them appeared to make remarks about me, as I passed through the crowd up the wharf; but so completely had my thoughts been absorbed by the affairs of my father, that I had quite forgotten my altercation with Mr. Waddie Wimpleton, and I did not connect the sharp looks and the suppressed remarks bestowed upon me with that circumstance. I had the young gentleman's revolver in my pocket; but I had ceased to feel its weight or to think of it. I walked up the wharf, and hastened to the cottage of my father.

"Why, Wolfert! What have you been doing?" exclaimed my mother, as I entered the kitchen, where she was at work.

"Nothing wrong, I hope, mother," I replied; and I am sure my long face and sad demeanor were not without their effect upon her.

"They are telling awful stories about you, Wolfert," she added.

"Who are?"

"Everybody. What have you been doing?"

"I haven't done anything, mother."

"Didn't you take the powder from the tool-house at the quarry, and blow up that canal boat?" gasped she, horrified that I should be even accused of such wickedness.

"No, mother; I did not. Who says I did?"

"Everybody is saying so. We all know that the canal boat was blown up; and they say you ran away before the people came."

I told my mother the whole truth in regard to the canal boat, and she believed me.

"Waddie Wimpleton says you did it, Wolfert," added she.

"I did not do it, and did not know anything about it till the explosion took place."

"They all say you must have done it. Waddie don't deny that he had a hand in it; but he says you planned the whole thing, and he gave you his revolver for doing it."

"There is not a word of truth in it, mother."

"The quarrymen saw you and Waddie near the mill wharf, just before the explosion. It was not till they had told their story that Waddie acknowledged he had anything to do with it. He says it was done by pulling a string; and everybody believes that boy hadn't gumption enough to blow up the canal boat without blowing himself up with it. They say the thing was well done, and therefore you must have done it."

This was flattering to my pride, disagreeable as the consequences threatened to be. People believed I was guilty because I had the reputation of being skilful in mechanical contrivances! But I was not anxious to rob Waddie of any of his honors in this affair.

"I have not done anything wrong, mother; and I am willing to take the consequences, whatever they are. I wish this was the only thing we had to fear," I said, dreading the effect upon her of the intelligence I had to communicate in regard to my father.

"Why, what else have we to fear?" asked she, with an expression of alarm. "Where is your father?"

"He has gone up to Hitaca in the steamer."

"What has he gone up there for?"

"He is in charge of the engine of the Ruoara."

"Where is Christy Holgate?"

"He has robbed a man of his money, and run away."

"Christy?"

"Yes, mother; and that isn't the worst of it, either."

"Why, what do you mean, Wolfert?"

"Father was the man whom he robbed."

"Why, Wolfert!" ejaculated my mother, as pale as death.

"It is just as I say, mother; and it isn't the worst of it, either."

"Oh, dear! What else has happened?" she demanded, in a hoarse whisper.

"Father has taken to drinking again," I replied; and, no longer able to restrain my emotions, I burst into tears.

"Merciful Heaven! That is worse than all the rest!" exclaimed she, covering her face with her apron, and weeping bitterly with me.

CHAPTER X.

COLONEL WIMPLETON AND SON.

MY mother wept as she thought of the past, and dreaded the future. It would have been comparatively easy to endure the loss of the twenty-four hundred dollars; but it was intolerable to think of the misery of again being a drunkard's wife. All else was as nothing to her beside this awful prospect. My father had struggled with his besetting and his besotting sin for five years, and with hardly an exception had always been the conqueror. During this period he had prospered in his worldly affairs, and till this day of disaster the future seemed to be secure to him.

My mother told me I had done right in emptying the bottle, and assured me that my father would not long cherish his anger. She knew not what to do in order to turn the tide which had set against us. If the sheriff succeeded in arresting Christy, and securing the money he had stolen, the effect upon my father would be good. If the money was lost, we feared that father would be lost with it.

While we were talking about the sad prospect before us, an imperative knock was heard at the front door — a summons so loud and stately that we could hardly fail to identify the person even before we saw his face. My mother wiped away her bitter tears, and hastened to the door.

"Has your son come home?" demanded Colonel Wimpleton, in his abrupt and offensive manner, when he spoke to his social inferiors, as he regarded them.

"Yes, sir, he has," replied my mother, with fear and trembling before the magnate of Centreport.

Without further ceremony, or any ceremony, — for he had used none, — he stalked into the kitchen where I sat. He was followed by his hopeful scion, who looked quite as magnificent as his stately father.

"So you have come home, you young villain!" said the colonel, fixing a savage gaze upon me.

"I have come home; but I am not a villain, sir," I replied, with what dignity I could command.

"Don't contradict me. I say you are a villain."

"Your saying so don't make it so," I answered, desperately; for I was goaded almost to despair by the misfortunes of the day; and though at any other time I should have been as meek as a nursing dove, I felt like defending myself from the charges he was about to make.

"Don't be impudent to me, young man," scowled he. "You know me, and you know what I am."

"I know what you are," I added, significantly; and I was astonished at my own boldness.

He looked at me savagely, apparently trying to determine what construction to put upon my remark. Waddie stood at his side, quite self-possessed, considering the wicked deed he had done. His presence reminded me of the revolver I had in my pocket, and I took it out and presented it to him.

"Here is your revolver, Waddie. I did not intend to keep it, when I took it," said I.

"I don't want it. It is yours now," replied he,

declining to take the weapon. " I gave it to you for the job you did for me, and I am not going to back out now."

" Take it, Waddie," interposed his father. " Such a trade is not legal or binding."

" I'm not going to take it," replied the hopeful, stoutly. " It was a fair trade, and it would not be honorable for me to back out."

" Give it to me, then," added the colonel.

I gave it to him, and he put it in his pocket, in spite of the protest of Waddie.

" Now, Wolf, I want you to tell me the truth," continued Colonel Wimpleton.

" I will do so, sir."

" You persuaded my boy to blow up that canal boat?"

" No, sir. I did not."

" I didn't say he persuaded me to do it, father," interrupted the son.

" You wouldn't have done such a thing as that unless somebody put you up to it, Waddie," protested the fond father, who had been obliged to make the same statement fifty times before, and remained obstinately incredulous in regard to his son's capacity to do mischief up to the present time.

"Yes, I would, father; and I am only sorry the skipper of the canal boat was not on board when she went up. Didn't I say he insulted me? Didn't I tell you he shook me, kicked me, cuffed me, and then chucked me on the wharf, as though I had been a dead cat? When a man insults me, he has to pay for it," said Waddie, shaking his head to emphasize his strong declarations.

"Yes; and I shall have to pay for it too," muttered the colonel, who felt very much as the man did who had to pay his wife's fine after he had prosecuted her for an assault upon himself.

"No matter for that; I am revenged," added Waddie, coolly. "I only said that Wolf showed me how to do it, and pulled the string when all was ready."

"That's enough," replied the father.

I understood the magnate of Centreport well enough to comprehend his position. He was quite willing to pay a couple of thousand dollars for the destruction of the canal boat; but he was very loath to have the Centreporters believe, what was literally the truth, that Waddie Wimpleton was the worst and most evil-disposed boy in the whole town. While he did not attempt to discipline and control his vicious heir, he was exceedingly jealous of the youth's reputation. He wished to have me confess that I had had a finger in this pie of mischief. My character stood high in town, for I had tried to behave like a gentleman on all occasions. If I shared the blame with the colonel's hopeful, he was willing to pay all costs and damages. I really believe, if I could have assumed the entire odium of the wicked deed, the magnate would have been willing to pay for the boat, and give me a thousand dollars besides. In fact, I knew of one instance in which a boy of bad habits had been indirectly paid for taking upon his own shoulders the blame that belonged upon Waddie's.

"I had nothing at all to do with blowing up the canal boat, Colonel Wimpleton," I replied. "I knew nothing about it till the explosion took place."

"You deny it — do you?" demanded the magnate, sharply.

"I do, sir; I had nothing to do with it."

"How dare you lie to me? As Waddie was concerned in the affair, I don't mind paying for the boat, and I suppose that will be the end of the scrape; but I know my boy wouldn't do such a thing without some help."

"I didn't help him," I protested, warmly.

"Didn't you pull the string?" demanded Waddie, with the most unblushing effrontery.

"No, I did not."

"Didn't you have hold of the string when the boat went up?" persisted the young villain.

"I did, but" —

"There, father, he owns up to all I ask him to confess," interposed Waddie.

"I own up to nothing," I replied, indignantly. "I say, again, I had nothing to do with the explosion, and knew nothing about it till the boat blew up."

"What do you mean, you young rascal?" stormed the colonel. "One moment you say you had hold of the string, and the next that you knew nothing about it."

"If you wish me to explain the matter, I will do

so ; if not, I won't," I added, disgusted with the evident intention of the magnate to convict me, whether guilty or not.

" Will you confess that you had a hand in the mischief ? "

" No, I will not."

" But, you young rascal " —

" I am not a rascal, Colonel Wimpleton. If either of us is a rascal, you are the one, not I," I continued, goaded to desperation by his injustice.

" What ! " gasped the great man, confounded at my boldness.

" I say just what I mean. Waddie knows, as well as I do, that I had nothing to do with blowing up the canal boat, and if he was a decent fellow he would say so."

" Don't be rash, Wolfert," interposed my mother, alarmed at my temerity.

" I am not afraid of them, mother."

" Do you mean to say I'm not a decent fellow? " howled Waddie.

" I did say so, and I meant to say so. You know that you lie when you say I had anything to do with blowing up the boat."

"Do you tell me I lie?"

"I do; I tell you so with all my might," I persisted, boldly.

"We'll see about this," said Colonel Wimpleton, furiously. "Mrs. Penniman, your boy is impudent — impudent to me, and to my son."

"You accuse him of something he didn't do, and won't hear what he has to say," replied my mother, meekly.

"Accuse him of what he didn't do! Didn't he say he had hold of the string? Wolf had the pistol, too, and that proves the truth of what Waddie said. How came you by the pistol?" demanded the magnate, turning fiercely to me.

"I took it away from Waddie when he threatened to shoot me with it, and after he had fired one ball at me."

"Do you want to make it out that my boy intended to murder you? Once more, will you confess to me, or will you have it proved before a justice?"

"I don't care where you prove it; but I shall not confess what I didn't do."

"My son speaks the truth, Mrs. Penniman, though he may be a little wild sometimes."

"There isn't a bigger liar in town," said I, very imprudently.

"Do you hear that, marm?" snapped the colonel. "Didn't my son confess that he had a hand in the mischief? Doesn't that show that he is a truthful boy? Wolf is violent and abusive. I have done what I could for your family, Mrs. Penniman."

"I know you have, Mr. Wimpleton, and we are all very grateful to you," replied my trembling mother.

"I should think you were! You permit this young rascal to insult and abuse me and my son. He calls me a rascal, and my son a liar. Is that his gratitude?" continued the much-abused great man. "You will hear from me again, Mrs. Penniman."

"And you will hear from me again, Wolf Penniman. I don't allow any fellow to call me a liar," added Waddie, bristling up like a bantam rooster.

"You permit this young cub to insult and abuse me," persisted the magnate, as he bolted out of the front door, followed by his hopeful, who could not help shaking his fist at me as he went out.

"What have you done, Wolf?" exclaimed my mother, when they had gone.

"I have spoken the truth, like a man," I replied, though I trembled for the consequences of my bold speech to the great man.

"He will discharge your father; and, now the money is gone, he will turn us out of house and home," added my mother, beginning to cry again.

"I can't help it. I have only told the truth, and I am not going to cower before that man and that boy any longer."

I took my cap and left the house.

CHAPTER XI.

BETTER THOUGHTS AND DEEDS.

I LEFT the house more to conceal my own emotions than for any other reason. I had been imprudent. My father was not only dependent upon Colonel Wimpleton for the excellent situation he held, which had enabled him to live well, to give me a good education, and to save money to buy his place, though there was a mortgage on the little estate that would expire in a few days; so far as liberality in financial matters was concerned, no one could find any fault with the magnate of Centreport.

I was accused of a crime — not merely of a piece of mischief, as the colonel was pleased to regard it, but of a crime whose penalty was imprisonment. By merely admitting the truth of the charge, I could escape all disagreeable consequences, and retain for my father and myself the favor of the mighty man in whose smile we had prospered and grown rich. Doubtless, in the worldly sense, I had been very imprudent. It would have been safer for me not to deny the accusation, and not to resent the hard names applied to me.

As a matter of policy, I had always permitted Waddie to have his own way in his dealings with me. If he ordered me to do anything, I did it. If he called me names, I did not retort upon him. It galled me sorely to permit the puppy to ride over me in this manner; to be insulted, kicked, and cuffed at his royal pleasure; but while it was simply a sacrifice of personal pride, or even of self-respect, it did not so much matter. When, however, Waddie and his father wished to brand me as a criminal, and to browbeat me because I would not confess myself guilty of a deed in which I had no hand, my nature revolted. In my indignation, I had made use of some expressions which I had better not have used, and which I should not have used if I had not been suffering under the weight of that sad day's trials.

I did not care for myself under the displeasure of

the mighty man. My mother was a timid woman, and the cloud of misfortunes which was rising over us filled her with dismay. The displeasure of Colonel Wimpleton, the loss of the money, and above all the fear that my father would return to his old habits, were terrors enough for one day, and I wept for her. But what could I do? To confess myself guilty of a crime when I was innocent was the greatest wrong I could do to her and to myself. I would not do that, whatever else I did; and there was no other way to win back the favor of the colonel.

After I had cooled off, I returned to the house, and found my mother more calm than I expected. She had resumed her work; but she looked very sad and troubled. My two sisters had gone to the village, and as yet knew nothing of the misfortunes that were settling down upon our house.

"Wolfert, I am sorry you were so rash," said my mother, as I seated myself in the kitchen.

"I am sorry myself; but I don't think it would have made any difference with the colonel if I had been as gentle as a lamb," I replied.

" Perhaps it would."

" The colonel wished me to take upon my shoulders the blame, or part of it, of blowing up the canal boat. Nothing less than that would have satisfied them. You can't wonder that I was mad, after what you heard him say to me. I have eaten dirt before the colonel and his son for years, and I don't think we have made anything by it; but whether we have or not, I won't be called a villain and a scoundrel, or confess a thing I didn't do."

" Mr. Wimpleton is a very powerful man in Centreport," added my mother, shaking her head in deprecation of any rash steps.

" I know he is, mother; and I will do anything I can to please him, except sell my own soul; and he hasn't got money enough to buy that. I'm not going to put my nose into the dirt for him."

" He may ruin us, Wolfert."

" What can he do ? "

" He can discharge your father."

" Father can get as much wages in another place as he can here. Perhaps he will be wanted on the Ruoara, now Christy has run away."

"But his house is here, and he meant to stay in Centreport. Besides, Mr. Wimpleton can turn us out of the house if we don't pay the money, which will be due in a few days."

"I hope Mr. Mortimer will catch Christy, and get the money. If he don't, there is a man in town who offered thirty-five hundred dollars for the place; and that is more than it cost, and father won't lose anything."

"You don't know Mr. Wimpleton, Wolfert. He is a terrible man when he is offended. If the place were sold at auction, as it would be, he has influence enough to prevent any one from bidding on it; and your father might lose every cent he has left in the world."

"What would you have me do, mother?" I asked, rising from my chair, considerably excited. "Shall I say that I helped Waddie blow up the canal boat?"

"No, certainly not, Wolfert, unless you did help him."

"Do you think I did, mother?"

"No, I can't think so, after what you have said."

"I had nothing more to do with it than you had."

"But you can be a little more gentle with him."

"And let him browbeat and bully me as much as he pleases? I think, mother, if I stand up squarely for my own rights, he will respect me all the more. For my own part, I am about tired of Centreport, for all the people bow down and toady to Colonel Wimpleton. If he takes snuff, everybody sneezes. All the fellows treat Waddie as though he was a prince of the blood. I have been ashamed and disgusted with myself a hundred times after I have let him bully me and put his foot on my neck. I have been tempted to thrash him, a dozen times, for his impudence; and if I didn't do so, it was not because I didn't want to."

"You must try to have a Christian spirit, Wolfert," said the mother, mildly.

"I do try to have a Christian spirit, mother. I haven't anything against Waddie or his father. If I could do a kindness to either one of them this minute, I would do it. But I don't think a fellow must be a milksop in order to be a Christian. I don't think the gospel requires me to be a toady, or even to submit to injustice when I can help myself. I don't ask to be revenged, or anything of that sort; I only desire to keep my head out of the dirt. I am going to try to be a man, whatever happens to me."

"If you will only be a Christian, Wolfert, I can ask no more."

"I will try to be; but do you think yourself, mother, that I ought to stand still and allow myself to be kicked?"

"You must not provoke your enemies."

"I will not, if I can help it; but I think it is pretty hard to keep still when you are called a rascal and a villain. If you think I ought to confess that I helped blow up the canal boat when I did not, I will"—

I was going to say I would do it, but the words choked me, and I could not utter them.

"I don't wish you to say so, Wolfert."

"Then I am satisfied; and I will try to be gentle while they abuse me."

At this moment Waddie Wimpleton bolted into

the room, without taking the trouble to announce himself beforehand.

"My father says you must come up and see him at once," said the scion in his usual bullying and offensive tone.

"Where is he?" I asked, as quietly as I could speak, under the influence of my good mother's lesson.

"At the house. Where do you suppose he is?" pouted Waddie. "And he says, if you don't come, he'll send a constable after you."

"What does he want of me?"

"None of your business what he wants. All you've got to do is to go."

"If I conclude to go, I will be there in a few moments," I added.

"If you conclude to go!" exclaimed Waddie. "Well, that is cool! Do you mean to say you won't go?"

"No, I don't mean to say that."

"Well, I want to know whether you are going or not," demanded the scion.

"Shall I go, mother?" I asked, appealing to her.

"I think you had better go, Wolfert."

"Then I will go."

"You had better," continued Waddie, who could not help bullying even after his point was gained.

The gentlemanly young man left the house, and my mother admonished me again not to be saucy, and to return good for evil. I hoped I should be able to do so. If I failed, it would not be for the want of a good intention. I walked up the road towards the mansion of the great man, thinking what I should say, and how I could best defend myself from the charge which was again to be urged against me. The situation looked very hopeless to me as I jumped over the fence in the grove, through which there was a path which led to the house of the colonel.

"Here he is," said Waddie, accompanying the remark with a yell not unlike an Indian war-whoop.

I halted and turned around. Behind me stood the scion of the great house of Centreport, with a club in his hand, and attended by half a dozen of the meanest fellows of the Institute, armed in like manner. They had been concealed behind the fence;

and of course I instantly concluded that the colonel's message was a mere trick to decoy me into
the grove.

"Do you wish to see me?" I asked as coolly as
I could; and the circumstances under which we
appeared to meet were not favorable to a frigid
demeanor.

"Yes, I want to see you," replied Waddie, moving up to me, and flourishing his stick. "You must
settle my account before you see my governor."

"What do you want of me?" I demanded, as I
edged up to a big tree, which would protect me
from an assault in the rear.

"You told my father I was the biggest liar in
town," blustered Waddie. "I'm going to give you
the biggest licking for it you ever had in your life."

"Go in, Waddie!" shouted Sam Peppers. "We'll
stand by, and see fair play."

"Are you ready to take your licking?" bullied
Waddie, who did not seem to be quite ready to com-
mence the operation.

"No, I am not," I answered, quietly; and I never
spoke truer words in my life.

"You called me the biggest liar in town — didn't you?"

"I did."

"Have you anything to say about it?"

"I have," I replied, still moved by the gentle words of gospel wisdom which my mother had spoken to me.

"If you have, say it quick."

"I was angry when I spoke the words, and I am sorry for uttering them."

"Ha, ha! humph!" yelled the half-dozen ruffians in concert.

"Get down on your knees and beg my pardon, then," said Waddie.

"No, I will not do that," I replied, firmly.

CHAPTER XII.

WOLF'S FORTRESS.

UNDER the influence of the better thoughts which my good mother had suggested to me, I was willing to do better deeds. I was ready to apologize; I had done so, but I could not go down upon my knees before such a fellow as Waddie Wimpleton, or any fellow, for that matter. It was hard enough for me to say I was sorry; and I had done so for my mother's sake, rather than my own.

"I don't think you are very sorry for what you said," sneered Waddie.

"I am sorry enough to apologize. I really regret that I made use of any hard expressions," I replied.

"Then get down on your knees, and beg my pardon, as I tell you," persisted Waddie, flourishing his stick. "If you do, I'll let you off on part of the punishment."

"I apologized because I had done wrong, and not because I was afraid of the punishment," I added, still schooling my tongue to gentle speech.

"Humph!" exclaimed the scion; and my remark was based on a philosophy so subtle that he could not comprehend it.

"Go in! Go in! Give it to him!" shouted the supporting ruffians. "He's fooling you, Waddie."

"If you are not going to do what I tell you, look out for the consequences," blustered the young gentleman, who still seemed to have some doubts in regard to the prudence of his present conduct.

"Waddie Wimpleton," said I.

"Well, what do you want now?" demanded he, dropping his weapon again.

"If you strike me with that stick, you must look out for consequences. I shall defend myself as well as I know how."

Waddie glanced at his companions.

"Hit him! What are you waiting for?" cried his friends; and I have always observed, in such cases, that it is easier to give advice than to strike the blow.

Mr. Waddie had placed himself in a position which he could not well evacuate. He evidently had no heart for the encounter which he foresaw must take place if he struck me, and perhaps he had not entire confidence in the character of the support which he was to receive. At any rate he could not help realizing that the first blows of the battle were likely to be dealt upon his own head.

"You called me a liar," said he, working up his courage again by a new recital of his wrongs.

"I did, and apologized for it," I replied.

"Go down on your knees, then, and say you are sorry."

"I will not."

"Then mind your eye," continued Waddie, as with a sudden spring he hit me on the arm, which I had raised to ward off the blow.

I did mind my eye, and I minded his, too; for, before he could bring up his supports, I leaped upon him. Though he was of my own size and age, he was only a baby in my hands. I grasped his stick, wrenched and twisted it a few times, and then threw him over backwards into a pool of soft mud, which

9

I had chosen to flank my position and save me from an attack in the rear. He was half buried in the soft compound of black mud and decayed leaves which filled the hole, and his good clothes suffered severely from the effects of his disaster.

The moment the conflict commenced the supports moved up; but, before they could come into action, I had overthrown my assailant, and stood against the tree with the club in my hand. When Waddie went over backwards, a new duty seemed to be suggested to his backers; and, instead of turning on me, they proceeded to help their principal out of his uncomfortable position. Encouraged and thoroughly waked up by my victory, I think I could have thrashed the whole party; but I had not wholly escaped the influence of my mother's teachings, and was disposed to act strictly in self-defence.

The quagmire into which Waddie had fallen was near the bank of the brook which meandered through the grove, and which had been bridged in several places, as well to add to the convenience of passers-by, as to increase the picturesque beauty of the place. I deemed it best to retreat to one of these bridges, which was not more than three feet wide, and which would enable me to defend myself from an assault to the best advantage.

"Humph! you cowards!" snarled Waddie, as his companions lifted him out of the slough, and he spit out the mud and water which filled his mouth. "Why didn't you stand by me, as you promised?"

"We expected you to make a better fight than that," replied one of them; and it was doubtful to me whether they could assign any good reason why they had not stood by him.

"I did the best I could, and you did not come near me. I'm in a pretty pickle," sputtered Waddie, as he glanced at his soiled garments.

"We'll give it to him yet," said one of the party, as he glanced at me securely posted on the bridge.

"Where is he?" asked Waddie.

I was pointed out to him, and the sight of me inflamed all his zeal again.

"Come on, fellows; and stand by me this time. I wish I had my revolver here."

I was very glad he had not that formidable weapon about him, though I don't think he could have hit

me if he had fired at me; but he sometimes struck
the mark by accident. Waddie took a club from the
hand of one of his supporters, and rushed towards
the bridge. Though he was not a master of strategy,
he could not help seeing that I was well posted, and
he halted suddenly before he reached the brook.

"We must drive him from the bridge, where we
can have fair play," said Waddie.

I did not just then see how this was to be done;
but I was soon able to perceive his plan. The scion
led his forces to a position on the brook above me,
and, taking some stones from the shallow stream,
began to pelt me with a vigor which soon rendered
my place untenable. Several of the missiles hit me,
though I was not much hurt by them. Under these
circumstances, I was helpless for defensive purposes,
for I had nothing with which to return the fire. It
was useless for me to stand there, and be peppered
with stones. I concluded to retreat in good order,
and brought myself off without any material damage.

The only safe line by which I could retire was in
the direction of the mansion of Colonel Wimpleton.
I crossed the brook farther down, and came to a

CHAMPNEY

WOLF'S FORTRESS. — Page 183.

rustic summer house, on the bank of the stream. It was built on a high foundation, to afford a prospect of the lake, and the only admission was through the door, which was reached by a long flight of steps. I immediately took possession of this structure, assured that I could defend the door, while its walls would protect me from the missiles of my assailants.

Waddie led his forces up to my fortress, and surveyed the situation. They attempted to drive me out with stones; but they fell harmless upon the building. The besiegers consulted together, and decided to make an assault on the works. I was entirely willing they should do so, for I could knock them over with the club as fast as they came up, having all the advantage of position. Ben Pinkerton volunteered to lead the forlorn hope, and advanced with considerable boldness to the attack. I gave him a gentle rap on the head as he appeared at the door, and he fell back, unable to reach me with his stick, as I stood so much higher than he.

"Better keep back," I remonstrated with him. "If there are any broken heads, they will be yours."

Dick Bayard then attempted to climb up the railing of the stairs, so as to be on a level with me; but I knocked his fingers with my stick, and he desisted. It was plain to them, after this trial, that a direct assault was not practicable, and they retired to the ground below. Another consultation followed in the ranks of the enemy; and by this time Waddie's friends were quite as much interested in the affair as he was himself.

"I wish I had my revolver," said the scion. "Hold on! I will go to the house and get it; you stay here, and don't let him come down."

"Oh, no! We don't want any pistol," protested Ben Pinkerton. "You mustn't shoot him!"

"Why not? I would shoot him as quick as I would a cat. I wouldn't kill him, of course; but I would make him come down, and give us fair play on the ground," added Waddie.

Fair play! Seven of them, armed with clubs, against one! That was Waddie's idea of fair play.

"No; we don't want any pistols," persisted Ben. "Some one might get hurt, and then we should be in a bad scrape."

"What are you going to do?" demanded the young gentleman. "Are you going to let him stay up there and crow over us? I'm wet through, and I don't want to stay here all day. I'll tell you what I'll do. I'll set the summer house on fire. That will bring him down."

This was a brilliant idea of Waddie, and I was afraid he would put it into operation, for he was reckless enough to do anything.

"That won't do," replied the prudent Pinkerton. "We don't want to get into any scrape."

"No; don't set it on fire," added Dick Bayard; and so said all of them but Waddie; for probably they foresaw that they would have to bear all the blame of the deed.

"I don't want to stay here all day," fretted Waddie.

"Put it through by daylight!" I ventured to suggest, as I sat on the upper step, listening to the interview.

"He is laughing at us," said the scion, angrily.

"Let him laugh; he is safe," replied Ben. "I'll tell you what we can do."

"Well, what?" asked Waddie, as he cast a discontented glance at me.

" Let us camp out here to-night," continued Ben.

" Camp out !" repeated several of the party, not fully comprehending the idea of the fertile Pinkerton's brilliant mind.

" Starve him out, I mean," explained Ben. " We will stay here and keep him a close prisoner till he is willing to come down and take his licking like a man."

Stupid as this plan seemed to me, it was promptly adopted. But the enemy retired out of hearing to complete the arrangement, though they were near enough to fall upon me if I attempted to escape. I did not consider myself a match for the whole of them on the ground, and I had expected to be terribly mauled, as I should have been if my wits had not served me well.

Presently I saw Waddie leave the party, and walk towards his father's house. I concluded that he had gone to change his clothes, for his plight was as disagreeable as it could be. His companions took position near the foot of the steps, with the clubs in their hands, ready to receive me if I attempted to evacuate my fortress. I was quite comfortable, and rather curious to know what they intended to do.

I waited an hour for the return of Waddie, during which time I studied the structure in which I was a prisoner, and its surroundings, in order to prepare myself for action when it should be necessary. It was plain to me that the scion was taking more time than was needed to change his clothes. I thought something had happened at the house; and in this impression I was soon confirmed by the appearance of Colonel Wimpleton, attended by two men.

CHAPTER XIII.

CAPTAIN SYNDERS.

THERE were not many men in Centreport who were not either the toadies or the employees of Colonel Wimpleton. He was an absolute monarch in the place, and his will was law, to all intents and purposes, though of course he did not operate with all as he did with me. Ordinarily, and especially when not opposed, he was a very gentlemanly man, affable to his equals, — if he had any equals in town, — and condescending to his inferiors.

I was not quite willing to believe that Waddie had called upon his father for aid. It was more probable that the scion's dirty plight had attracted the attention of his parents, and called forth an explanation. But it was all the same to me, since Colonel Wimpleton was coming with efficient aid to capture and reduce me to proper subjection. It was no common enemy with whom I was called upon to contend, but the mighty man of Centreport, whose will none dared to oppose.

As the party approached, I saw that one of the men was Captain Synders, the ex-skipper of a canal boat, who had been promoted to the honors and dignities of a constable. I was somewhat appalled when I considered his official position, for he was armed with authority, and it would be hardly safe for me to offer any resistance to him. The coming of Colonel Wimpleton nipped in the bud the scheme of the bullies to camp out around me, and I was rather glad to have the case settled without any unnecessary delay.

The summer house, which was a poor imitation of an Indian pagoda, mounted on piles, had a door, with a window in each of its octagonal faces. On the other side of the brook was a large tree, whose branches partially shaded the building. During my study of the situation, I had arranged a plan by which my escape could be effected at a favorable moment. I could pass out at one of the windows, and climb to the roof of the pagoda, from which the overhanging branches of the trees would afford me the means of reaching the ground. The only difficulty in my way was, that my besiegers would be able to reach the foot of the tree before I could, and thus cut off my retreat. But the summer house was located near the lake, and the brook at this point was wide and deep, so that it could not be crossed except on the bridge, which was several rods distant. My line of retreat would be available only when the besiegers were off their guard, or were not in a situation to pursue instantly.

When Colonel Wimpleton appeared, Waddie's six brave companions retired from the ground, fearful, perhaps, of getting into a scrape. I saw them move off a short distance, and halt to observe the proceedings. The great man and his associates devoted their whole attention to me, and did not heed the students. They came directly to the foot of the stairs, while I sat at the head of them. I had made a movement to retire when the valiant six retreated; but I saw that the attempt would only throw me into the hands of the reënforcements.

"Come down, you villain!" called Colonel Wimpleton, as he halted at the foot of the stairs.

To this summons to surrender I made no reply.

"What do you mean by knocking my son over into the mud?" he added, angrily.

"He began it upon me, sir," I replied. "He brought up half a dozen fellows to lick me, and struck me with a club."

"He served you right. I told you to come down."

"I know you did, sir."

"Are you coming down?"

"Not just yet."

"Go up and bring him down, Synders," said the colonel to the officer.

"I'll bring him down," replied the zealous constable.

But he did not.

I sprang to my feet, leaped out upon the trimmings of the pagoda, and vaulted to the roof almost in the twinkling of an eye — at any rate, before Captain Synders reached the inside of the summer house. The constable looked out of the window at my elevated position. He was too clumsy to follow me, and I felt that I was perfectly safe. From the roof I saw that the branches of the tree were more favorable to my descent than I had supposed, and I found that I could climb into another tree on the same side of the brook as the pagoda. I jumped into the branches of this tree, and began to move down. I found that my gymnastic practice at the Institute, where I had excelled in this department, was of great service to me, and I was quite sure that no man could follow me.

Perching myself on a branch, I paused to examine the situation again. Captain Synders sent the man who had come with him, and who was one of the gardeners, to the foot of the tree to intercept my retreat. I did not purpose to go down that way, but intended, at the right time, to return to the roof of the pagoda, and descend on the other side of the brook. My movement in this direction was only a feint. The colonel expected, doubtless, that I would drop down into the arms of the gardener, and that the chase would be immediately ended; but, seated on the branch, I kept still, and said nothing.

"Are you going down, you scoundrel?" roared the colonel, when he found the plan did not work.

"No, sir, not yet."

"You are on my grounds, and I will have you arrested as a trespasser," foamed the colonel.

"You sent for me, sir, and I came at your request."

"Who sent for you?"

"You did, sir; ask Waddie; he was your messenger."

"I didn't send for you."

"Waddie came to my house, and said you wanted to see me."

"I want to see you now, at any rate."

"Here I am, sir."

"You shall be punished for knocking my son over into the mud."

"I would like to talk this matter over coolly, Colonel Wimpleton," I continued, taking an easy position in the tree. "I apologized to Waddie for calling him a liar, and I am sorry I was saucy to you."

" Humph ! Come down from that tree, then. **If** you make a clean breast of it, I will let you **off** easy."

" I don't think I'm to blame for anything except being saucy," I replied ; and I did not think I was much to blame for that, after he had called me a villain and a scoundrel, and other hard names ; still it was returning evil for evil.

" Did he apologize to you, Waddie ? " asked the colonel, turning to his hopeful.

" He said he was sorry, and I told him to get down on his knees and beg my pardon," replied Waddie.

" And he would not do it ? " asked the indignant father, evidently regarding it as exceedingly unreasonable in me to refuse to undergo this trifling humiliation.

" No, he wouldn't."

" Very well," replied the great man. " We shall see whether he will or not."

I was willing to see.

" Wolf Penniman, you are a bad boy ! " exclaimed the colonel with emphasis.

I did not dispute him.

"You have insulted me and my son."

"I am willing to be forgiven, sir," I answered, after a vain effort to keep down the spirit which was rising in me. "I have apologized for being saucy; what more can I do?"

"You must do what my son told you to do, and then confess that you helped blow up the canal boat," replied he, more calmly than he had yet spoken.

"I can't do anything more, then. I know nothing about the blow-up, and I won't go down on my knees to anybody in this world."

"You are an obstinate villain, and I'll bring you to your senses before I have done with you. Where is your father?"

"Gone to Hitaca."

"Will you come down now, or shall I have you brought down?"

"I'll be brought down, if it's all the same to you, sir," I replied, folding my arms, and looking as impudent as I spoke.

I felt that I had given my mother's good advice

10

a fair trial. I had gained nothing by apologizing, though I was not sorry I had done so. The more I humiliated myself, the more I must; and, without meaning to be saucy, I determined to stand up squarely for my own rights and my own dignity.

"I'll bring him down, if you say so, father," volunteered the Wimpleton junior.

"How?"

"We can drive him out of the tree, as we did off the bridge."

"Exactly so!" exclaimed Captain Synders. "That's a good idea. Since neither words nor grass will do, we'll try what virtue's in a stone or two."

The besiegers went down the stairs, and Waddie called up his forces, ready to renew the assault. By the time they reached the ground, I had descended to the roof of the pagoda, where the party could not see me, and where the thick branches of the trees protected me from their missiles. They soon found they were not getting ahead any, and by the advice of Synders they changed their position. With the exception of the colonel, who was too dignified to throw stones, men and boys renewed the assault, and poured a shower of stones upon me. Some of them hit me, and the roof became too warm for me. I dropped down into the summer house for safety. Finding the coast clear, — for the colonel had been forced to retire from the foot of the stairs to avoid the stones, — I rushed down the steps, and ran with all my might towards home. The besiegers had been careless, and I was only too happy to take advantage of their mistake.

I ran as fast as I could over the bridge, following the path by which I had come. I was closely pursued; but I distanced all my enemies. It would be useless for me to go home; for the constable was a man of authority, and I supposed he had been sent for to arrest me, though on what charge I could not conjecture, for Wimpleton senior would not dare to prosecute me in a matter wherein Wimpleton junior would be likely to suffer more than myself. I wished to spare my mother the pain and anxiety of another controversy in the house; and for that reason, as well as because home was not a safe place for me, I made my way to the mill wharf, where I had an old skiff.

I reached this boat without accident, but out of breath with the hard run I had had. Jumping in, I pushed off, and pulled away from the shore. For the present I was safe, for there was no boat in which I could be pursued, nearer than the mansion of Colonel Wimpleton. The constable and his companions did not come down to the wharf after they saw me push off, but returned in the direction of the grove. I rowed out upon the lake, where I could see any boat which might put off after me. I went half way across the lake, and then concluded that my assailants had chosen to wait for my return.

I did not exactly like to return then; it would only be putting my head into the lion's mouth; and I pulled for Middleport. A sail-boat was near me, in which were several boys, one of whom presently hailed me.

"Is that you, Wolf?" called the speaker, in whom I recognized Tommy Toppleton.

I informed him that it was I.

"I was going over after you," he added. "Jump aboard — will you?"

I did so, and was glad to find myself among friends, though they were Toppletonians.

"We want you to get that engine out of the water," continued Tommy.

I saw the tow-boat at the wharf, with steam up, and I promised to do the job before night — in fact, to put it through by daylight.

CHAPTER XIV.

RAISING THE DUMMY.

HAVEN'T you any one in Middleport that can raise that engine?" I asked, with a pleasant smile, after I had taken a seat in Tommy Toppleton's beautiful sail-boat, with my old skiff in tow.

"Of course we have," replied the Toppleton junior; but I'm afraid it will take a week for them to do it. They are talking about rigging a derrick on the wharf."

"You don't need any derrick, or anything of that sort," I added, confidently; and I was quite satisfied that with the aid of the tow-boat I could make good my promise.

"Do you think you can really raise the thing?" asked Tommy, anxiously.

"I know I can."

" Can you do it right up quick?"

" It may take an hour or so. Can I have your father's tow-boat?"

" Certainly you can; but my father don't know I came over after you," added the scion of the house of Toppleton.

" I don't want to do anything without your father's knowledge and consent."

" He won't find any fault with anything except that you are a Centreporter."

" I am no more a Centreporter than I am a Middleporter now," I replied. " I have had a row with the powers that be on our side."

" A row!   Good!" exclaimed Tommy, his face brightening up at this intelligence. " What was it?"

I explained what it was, telling the whole history of the blowing up of the canal-boat, with the collateral incidents relating to the affair.

" That's just like Wimpleton," said Tommy. " We don't behave in that way on our side of the lake."

I hoped they did not; but it was a fact patent to the people, that Mr. Tommy, though by no means as bad a boy as Waddie, was a spoiled child.

He was overbearing, domineering, and inclined to get into bad scrapes. Though he was willing to be my friend, and to treat me with the greatest consideration at the present time, it was only because he had an axe to grind; and I had not much confidence in the professions he made to me.

"I wish you would come and live on our side," added Tommy. "We want just such a fellow as you are over here."

"Perhaps I may have to live over here," I replied. "I suppose Waddie will not let me rest in peace after what has happened; and I never will go down on my knees to him or any other person."

"Don't you do it, Wolf," said Tommy, warmly. "If you want a dozen or twenty of our fellows to go over and whip out the crowd that set upon you, we will do it — won't we, fellows?"

"I'll bet we will," replied the half dozen particular cronies of Tommy who were in the boat with him.

"I don't wish to do anything of that kind. I bear Waddie no ill will; and if he will only let me alone, I shall never have any trouble with him."

" You are too easy with him. If you only licked him once, he would respect you for it."

I could not help thinking what the consequences would be if any plebeian Middleporter took it into his head to " lick " Tommy Toppleton; and it was about the same on one side of the lake as the other. It was not prudent to thrash so much pride, conceit, and wealth, as were embodied in the person of either of the heirs of the great houses. The sons of poor men had to stand back, and take off their hats to the scion of either family. Fathers' situations and mothers' social positions depended much upon the deference paid by their children to the representatives of the nabobs.

" Where shall I land you, Wolf ?" asked Tommy, as the sail-boat approached the wharf, near which the dummy reposed, ignominiously, on the bottom of the lake.

" Put me on board of the tow-boat, if you please. And you must get the captain to do what I tell him," I replied.

" I'll do that. He shall obey your orders just as though you were the owner of the steamer."

We ran up to the tow-boat, which was about to start on a trip up the lake with a fleet of canal boats that had gathered together. I knew that she had on board all the rigging I needed for my bold experiment, including some very long tow-lines. Tommy ran up to the boat, and he and I leaped upon her deck, for I had assured him I needed no help from the boys, or any one else.

"Captain Underwood, we want to use your boat for a while," said Tommy, as briskly as though he had himself been the owner of the craft.

"Does your father say so?" asked the captain, with some hesitation, and with the utmost deference.

"No matter whether he does or not; I will be responsible. Now go ahead, Wolf. You can put her through by daylight."

The captain consented to take part in the enterprise, when informed that I was the "young engineer," — as I had the honor to be called, — and that I had a plan to put the dummy on shore.

"Shall I explain the plan to you, Captain Underwood?" I asked.

"No, you needn't, Wolf, unless you wish to do so," interposed Tommy, impatiently.

"If you will tell me what to do, I will obey orders," answered the captain. "In fact, I don't care to know anything about it; and then I shall be responsible for nothing."

"All right, captain. You shall not be responsible, and if I fail no harm will be done. Have you a stout iron hook?"

"Yes; here is one on the end of this tow-line," he replied, pointing to a coil of large rope.

"That's just what I want," said I, throwing off my coat. "Now run up to the north side of the dummy."

Before the steamer reached the spot I had thrown off all my clothes. Jumping into my skiff with Tommy, who was proud and happy to have a finger in the pie, we took the tow-line on board, and pulled to the end of the dummy, to which I made fast. I had ascertained from my companion that there was a shackle eye in each end of the engine, by which another car could be attached to it; and my present purpose was to fasten the hook into this eye.

The water of Lake Ucayga is as clear as crystal, and I had no trouble in finding the eye, which was no more than four feet below the surface of the lake. I dropped down into the engine-room, standing up to my neck in water, and Tommy lowered down the iron hook. I then stooped down, disappeared from the view of the world above me for a moment, and attached the hook to the eye.

"All right, Tommy," said I, when I had cleared the water from my mouth.

"Bully for you, Wolf; but I don't see how you are going to put the thing on shore," replied he.

"I'm going to do it; if I don't I never will go on shore again myself," I added, as I sprang upon the roof of the dummy again.

"I should hate to fail, for the fellows are a-gathering on the wharf to see the fun."

"There's no such word as fail," I answered, leaping into the boat. "Now pull for the tow-boat, and let me put on my rags again."

I jumped upon deck, and in a few moments had my clothes on. I glanced at the wharf, and saw that quite a number of students and grown-up people had gathered there, as the intelligence spread that something was going on.

"What next, Wolf?" asked Captain Underwood, bestowing upon me a smile which seemed to indicate an utter want of confidence in my operations.

"Go ahead, captain," I replied, seizing the tow-line, and making it fast at the bits provided for the purpose.

I knew what the bottom of the lake was at the Middleport wharf, for I had been down there more than once. It was composed of hard gravel, and almost as smooth as the surface of the lake in a calm day. I knew that the flanges of the car wheels would cut into the ground and make it go hard and they would run as well there as on a hard road.

"Go ahead!" said Captain Underwood to the engineer.

"Steady, captain! Work her up gradually," I added.

The wheels turned slowly at first, so as not to part the tow-line, or needlessly wrench the sunken car; but in a few moments she had full steam on. It was an anxious moment to me, and the gathering crowd on shore watched the movement in silence.

"She starts!" exclaimed Tommy, highly excited. "She's coming!"

"Of course she's coming; I knew she would," I replied, struggling to keep down the emotions which agitated me.

"Hurrah!" yelled Tommy, as the dummy began to follow us, as though she were a part of the steamer.

"Starboard your helm, Captain Underwood," I called.

"Starboard it is," replied the captain, when he had given the order to the wheelman.

"Keep as well in shore as your draught will let you," I continued.

"I can't run the boat up on the shore, Wolf," said the captain.

"I don't want you to do so. The dummy travels very well on the bottom."

"Yes; but we can't drag it out of the water without running upon shore with the boat."

"I think we can, captain. At any rate, don't let the boat get aground," I replied.

The steamer continued on her course till she came

abreast of a large tree growing on the shore, between which and the lake the rails were laid down.

"Stop her!" I shouted; and my order was
promptly obeyed.

The dummy was now in about six feet of water,
and not more than a hundred feet from the tree.
It was headed in a diagonal towards the railroad.

"Now, Captain Underwood, have you a heavy
snatch-block?" I asked as the boat stopped.

"I have — one used with that tow-line," replied
the obliging captain, to whom the request indicated
the nature of further operations; and I ought to add,
in justice to him, that the look of incredulity which
had played upon his face was all gone.

I took the snatch-block, with the ropes to make it
fast, and the end of the tow-line, into the skiff, and,
attended by Tommy, pulled ashore. My companion,
in spite of the fact that he usually wore kid gloves,
made himself exceedingly serviceable. I rigged the
snatch-block to the tree, and passed the tow-line
over the sheaf, carrying the end back to the steamer
in the boat, where I made it fast to the stern bits.

"Go ahead, captain!" I called.

Working her up to her speed slowly and carefully, the steamer ploughed and strained for a few moments, then went ahead. The rope strained, but it did not part, and the dummy walked up out of the water as though she had been a sea-horse emerging from his native element.

The crowd which had followed the steamer cheered lustily, and my promise was redeemed.

CHAPTER XV.

GETTING UP STEAM.

THE enthusiastic cheering which followed the passage of the dummy from the water to the land was grateful to me, and I enjoyed it to a degree which I cannot express. I felt just as though the Centreporters had cast me out, and the Middleporters had taken me up. I was quite confident that there were many persons in Middleport who could have raised the dummy; but no one seemed to have thought of my plan. Perhaps few of them knew the bottom of the lake as well as I did, for diving was one of my accomplishments; and I had oftener gone into the water on the Middleport side than on the other, because the beach was better.

"By gracious, Wolf! you have done it!" exclaimed Tommy Toppleton, as I directed the captain to stop the steamer; and his mouth and his eyes were opened as wide as if an earthquake had rent the lake beneath us.

"Of course I have done it; I expected to do it," I replied, as indifferently as I could, for, however big one may feel, he does not always like to show it.

"You have done it handsomely, too," added Captain Underwood; and praise from Sir What's-his-name was praise indeed.

"I hope the Wimpleton fellows saw that," said Tommy, puffing out his cheeks, and looking as grand as an alderman. "It would take them down a peg if they did."

"I expect to catch it for helping you out," I added, as I thought of the wrath of Colonel Wimpleton, when he should hear that I had been playing into the hands of the Toppletonians.

"Don't you be afraid of the whole boodle of them," replied Tommy, shaking his head, as though he thought the other side would make a great mistake if it attempted to punish me for what I had done.

"We'll talk about that some other time," I answered, turning my attention to business again.

"We haven't quite done the work yet. We must put the dummy on the track."

"Can I help you any more?" asked the captain, with a deference which amazed me.

"You may give us one more pull, if you are not in a hurry. I'm going on shore now, and I will make a signal to start and to stop her, with my handkerchief," said I, jumping into the skiff with Tommy.

The dummy stood within a couple of rods of the track, which was in readiness as far as Spangleport, five miles down the lake. We landed, and marched in triumph through the crowd of men and boys on the shore, though I ought to say that Tommy did the triumphal part of the programme, and looked as grand as though he had himself been the engineer of the movement. Scores of the students offered their services, and as I was on the point of sending some of them for a few planks on which to roll the dummy to the track, a platform car, which had constituted the entire rolling stock of the Lake Shore Railroad, rumbled up to the spot, in charge of a portion of the students, attended by Major Toppleton himself. The car was loaded with planks and rigging, which the Middleport magnate had foreseen we should want.

"We've got her out, father!" shouted Tommy, when he saw the major.

"I see you have," replied the great man, with a cheerful smile.

"But we haven't quite finished the job yet," added the young gentleman, bustling about as though the completion of the work rested heavily on his shoulders. "What next, Wolf?" said he, turning to me, and speaking in a lower tone.

"We must lay down some planks to roll it on the track with," I replied.

"Bring up the planks, fellows!" cried Tommy; and the students rushed to obey his commands.

"This is Wolf — is it?" said Major Toppleton, bestowing a patronizing glance at me.

"Yes, father; this is Wolf, and he puts things through by daylight, I can tell you. He and I have managed this thing ourselves," replied Tommy, swelling with importance.

"I'm glad to see you, Wolf. They say you have a taste for machinery."

" Yes, sir ; I'm very fond of machinery."

" And you live on the other side ? "

" Yes, sir ; my father is the engineer in Colonel Wimpleton's steam mill."

" Humph ! " ejaculated the major. " But you have done well, for I was just offering a man two hundred dollars to raise the dummy. He said it would take him three days to rig his derrick, and bring down his capstans from Ucayga. I was talking with him when you hooked on and dragged the thing away. You are a smart boy."

" Thank you, sir."

" You shall not lose anything by the job, if you do belong on the other side," said the major, magnanimously.

" O, I don't ask anything, sir.   I only did it for fun."

" Well, it's good fun, at any rate," laughed the great man.   " The boys will think you are a little god."

" I suppose I shouldn't have dared to meddle with it if I had not fallen out with Colonel Wimpleton and his son."

"Ah, indeed?" queried the major, opening his eyes, as a gleam of satisfaction passed over his face. "We will talk that matter over when your job is finished."

By this time the students, who would have insulted me if I had come among them at any other time, had brought up the planks from the car, and I proceeded to lay a track for the dummy wheels. I placed two lines of wide ones as far as the iron rails, sweeping them in curves, so as to turn the engine as it neared the track. On them I laid narrower planks for the wheels to run upon, gauging them with a stick measured to the width of the flanges of the wheels. When all was ready for a start, I gave the signal with my handkerchief. The steamer paddled and splashed, the rope strained, and the dummy started again. I directed the students to steady the planks so that they should not slip, and in a couple of minutes, more or less, we had the machine on the temporary track I had rigged. I waved my handkerchief again, and the boat stopped.

"That will do, Tommy," said I. "Tell your fellows to cast off the snatch-block, and let the captain haul in his tow-line. We shall not want it any more."

"But the dummy is not on the track yet," replied Tommy, fearful that some delay might occur.

"We can move it on the planks easily enough without the steamer; and she pulls so hard I am afraid she will overdo the matter. Send a couple of your fellows off in my skiff with the snatch-block and ropes."

The scion of the Toppleton house liked to be "the biggest toad in the puddle," and he gave off his orders with great gusto to the students, not always in as gentlemanly terms as I could have wished, but with effect. He was promptly obeyed, without dispute. I suggested to him that the cushions and other movable articles in the passenger compartment of the dummy should be removed, and placed in the sun to dry. Tommy went at the students as though the idea was his own, and made all hands "stand around" for a moment. I was very willing to flatter his vanity by letting him do the ordering.

There was a brake in the engine-room, and another

on the platform in the rear of the car. Tommy, at my request, placed a student at each of them. I then rigged a long rope at the forward end of the dummy, which was manned by a crowd of boys, while the men who were standing by took hold at the sides and end of the car.

"Now start her, Tommy," said I in a low tone, so as to permit him to enjoy the pleasing illusion that he was running the machine.

"Now, all together — ahead with her!" shouted Tommy, flourishing his arms like the director of an orchestra.

"Steady, Tommy."

"Steady!" yelled my mouthpiece.

The dummy moved slowly forward, till the drive-wheels came to the iron track.

"Put on the brakes! Stop her!" shouted Tommy, as I gave him the word.

The passage of the wheels from the planks down to the iron track involved some difficulty; but, by the aid of rocks and a couple of iron bars, the transit was effected, and the dummy was safely deposited on the rails in just an hour after the work began.

"Three cheers for the Lake Shore Railroad!" shouted one of the students, in the violence of his enthusiasm, when the job was completed.

They were given with a will.

"Three more for Wolf Penniman," added another student; and I was duly complimented, for which I took off my cap and bowed my acknowledgments.

"Don't forget Tommy," I whispered to one of the fellows.

"Three rousing cheers for Tommy Toppleton," called the student to whom I had given the hint.

Perhaps some of them thought that Mr. Tommy had not done anything to entitle him to the consideration; but the cheers were given, and supplemented with a "tiger."

"Fellow-students, I thank you for this compliment, and for this evidence of your good will," said Tommy, taking off his hat. "I have done the best I could to help along the Lake Shore Railroad, and as the president of the company, I am much obliged to you for this token of encouragement. When our rolling stock was buried beneath the wave, it was my duty to do something; and I've done it. I'm glad you are satisfied with the result."

Then Tommy was the president of the Lake Shore Railroad Company! I did not know this before; his zeal was fully explained, and I was all the more pleased that I had permitted him to exercise the lion's share of the authority.

"Three cheers for Major Toppleton," squeaked a little fellow, who thought the magnificent patron of the enterprise had been neglected.

The great man bowed and smiled, as great men always do when they are cheered; but he did not take up any of our valuable time by making a speech.

"Tommy, we want some oil and some packing," I suggested to the president of the road, after I had examined the machinery of the dummy.

"Do you think you can start her up to-night, Wolf?" asked Tommy, anxiously, after he had despatched half a dozen of his satellites for the required articles.

"Certainly we can; you shall ride over to Spangle-port, and back to Middleport in her," I replied. "Now let some of your fellows bring up water to fill the boiler and the tank, and we will get up steam in the course of an hour or so."

The boys returned from the steam mill with packing and oil; and, while others were bringing wood and water, I rubbed up and oiled the machinery. Brooms, mops, and cloths were obtained, and, under Tommy's direction, the passenger portion of the car was cleaned and wiped. The engine had been well oiled before it was sent up from Philadelphia, and I had nothing to do but wipe off the water and lubricate the running parts. I kindled a fire in the furnace, and, when the smoke began to pour out of the smoke-stack, the students yelled for joy.

CHAPTER XVI.

THE FIRST TRIP OF THE DUMMY.

I WAS in my element — in charge of a steam-engine. Though I had never seen a dummy before this one, I comprehended the machinery at a glance. I hardly heard the tumultuous yells of the Toppletonians as they manifested their joy, so absorbed was I in the study of the machine, and in the anticipation of what wonderful things it would do. Such an excited crowd as that which surrounded me I had never seen, and I was obliged to close the door of the engine-room to keep them out. I opened it with due deference when Mr. Tommy Toppleton, the president of the Lake Shore Railroad, made a demand for admission, but I remorselessly excluded the board of directors and the superintendent, to their great mortification, no doubt; but I did not know them just then.

Tommy and his father were busily engaged in a conversation which seemed to relate to me, when I rang the bell to indicate that the engine was ready for a start. This announcement was greeted with the usual volley of cheers, and the young gentlemen began to pile into the passenger apartment to a degree which perilled the powers of the car. There were at least a hundred of them, and it was impossible to accommodate the whole. The major directed his son to divide them into two companies; and, though all of them manifested a childish impatience to have the first ride, they submitted to the arrangement. Fifty of them filled the car, and Major Toppleton and Tommy honored me with their company in the engine room.

" All aboard ! " shouted the president.

" I think they need no such invitation," I added, laughing.

" We must do things up in shape, you know. We are all ready now, Wolf," replied Tommy, highly excited.

" I don't know anything about the road on which I am to run, Mr. President," I suggested, as a preparation for any accident which might happen.

" The road is all right, you may depend upon that," answered Tommy.

" Of course, if the rails happen to be spread, or anything of that sort, we shall be thrown off the track."

" I sent a man over it with a gauge, yesterday, and he reported it to be in perfect condition," interposed the major. " It would be very unfortunate to have any accident happen, and I have taken every precaution to guard against one."

" I think we had better run very slowly the first time," I replied.

" You can't be too careful, young man."

" Let her drive, Wolf ! " said Tommy, impatiently.

I let off the brake, and opened the valve. The steam hissed in the most natural and encouraging manner, and the dummy began to move, amid the shouts of those on board and those on the ground. The road was very level and straight, and the car moved as easily as a boat in the water, though the engine made a disagreeable puffing and twanging noise in its action.

" Here we go ! " roared Tommy, at the top of his

THE FIRST TRIP OF THE DUMMY. Page 175.

lungs, swinging his cap to the boys who stood at the sides, looking in at the door. "This is bully!"

"Exceedingly bully!" laughed his father.

"I should like to run through some of the Wimpleton fellows about this time," added the president. "They would find out that our side of the lake is wide awake."

I did not care to present myself to the Wimpletonians just at that moment. If I had, I should have been mobbed as a traitor to my own side; though, after the treatment which Centreport, in the persons of its magnate and its magnate's son, had bestowed upon me, my conscience did not reproach me for infidelity. I had actually been driven out of the place, and the colonel had no right to expect anything different from me.

The dummy went along very smoothly, and worked so well that I ventured to "let her out" a little more. The outsiders, in their excitement, had followed us so far; but, as I let on the steam, we ran away from them, the outsiders giving a rousing cheer as we distanced them. The ground on which the road was laid was nearly a dead level, though in some places a shelf on the side hill on the border of the lake had been dug out. Between Spangleport and the other terminus, two bridges had been built over a couple of brooks, and the expense of constructing the road was little more than the cost of sleepers and rails.

In about half an hour we reached Spangleport, which consisted of a wharf, a store, and about a dozen houses, on the lake shore, though there was quite a large village a mile distant. The occupants of the dozen houses turned out in a body, as the dummy went hissing and sizzling on its way. The students yelled and cheered, and the Spangleporters manifested their enthusiasm in a proper manner. It was a great occasion for Spangleport, and both natives and visitors made the most of it during the few moments we remained.

As there was no turn-table, we were obliged to run to Middleport backwards; but one of the conductors was placed on the forward platform to keep a lookout, and as he could ring a bell in the engine-room by pulling the strap, the car could be stopped in an instant. But there were no road crossings or obstructions of any kind to bother us, and we went ahead at a high rate of speed, rushing through the crowd of students we had left where the dummy was raised, and stopping only when we reached Middleport.

The whole village turned out to greet the dummy when she appeared; but we left our freight, and immediately returned to take up the waiting party, who were impatiently anticipating their first ride on the machine. I was beginning to grow tired of yelling and cheering; for I was not disposed to be very demonstrative myself, and I hoped the novelty would soon wear off, so that we could move without seeming like a horde of wild Indians. Probably I did not enjoy the stirring events of the day as much as I should if I had no trouble on the other side of the lake; for, in spite of the excitement of running the dummy, I could not help thinking, occasionally, of my poor mother, who was wondering what had become of me. I dreaded to hear from my father, for I was afraid that he had renewed his drinking after I left the boat. It seemed to me just as though our happy family had been broken in pieces by the events of that day; and I could not shake off a certain degree of sadness that hung over me.

I stopped the engine when we came to the party of students who were waiting for us, and they piled in like a flock of sheep. Tommy shouted, "All aboard!" after he was positively sure that every fellow was in the car; and we went off again in the midst of a din of cheers and yells that would have beggared Bedlam.

"Let her slide now — can't you, Wolf?" said Tommy. "Make her spin!"

"I don't like to run her too fast, till she gets a little used to it," I replied.

"Are you afraid of her?"

"No; but it's all a new thing, and we must be careful, as your father said."

"Father isn't here, now," answered Tommy; for the young gentleman had insisted that the machine should be run by the boys alone on this trip.

"I don't want to smash you up, Mr. President; but I will obey orders."

"All right; let her slide."

I let her go as fast as I thought it was safe
for her to go; but I did not regard Tommy as a
very safe president. By this time I felt quite at
home on the engine; but I should have enjoyed it
more if I had been alone, for I did not like the
interference of my companion. I foresaw that, under
his direction, many risks must be run, and that it
would be difficult always to keep on the right side
of him. He was good-natured now, but I knew
very well that such was not his invariable habit.
Like Waddie Wimpleton, he was disposed to be
tyrannical and overbearing. He liked his own way
and it was not very pleasant to think of being his
dependent.

We ran up to Spangleport; and, after a vast
amount of cheering and yelling by the boys, and
a reasonable display of enthusiasm on the part of
the inhabitants, we started for the return. Tommy
wanted to go faster; and I was very much afraid
I should have a quarrel with him before night. Running backwards, I could not see anything ahead of
the dummy, and I had not entire confidence in the
lookout on the forward platform. Fortunately we

had not a large supply of fuel on board, and this afforded me a sufficient excuse for not getting up too much steam.

We ran into Middleport, where the rest of the students, and hundreds of men, women, and children were waiting to see more of the dummy. By this time it was well dried off, and all the varnished parts had been rubbed by the boys till it looked as good as new. A house had already been built for the engine, near the Institute. It was provided with a water cistern, from which the tanks in the engine could be filled, and with other conveniences for taking care of it.

When the people had examined the car to their satisfaction, I ran it into the engine-house, put out the fire, and placed the machinery in proper order for use the next day. My work for that occasion was done, and I felt that I had "put her through by daylight."

"Now, Wolf, father wants to see you at the house," said Tommy, when I had finished my task on the engine.

"What does he want of me?" I asked, curiously.

"Oh, he wants to see you," answered the young gentleman; and he deemed this a sufficient reason why I should do as I was asked.

I followed Tommy to the great mansion, and was ushered into the library, where the major was reading the newspapers which had just come by the mail.

"Well, Wolf, I'm glad to see you," said the magnate of Middleport, laying aside his paper. "You have done more than a man's work to-day, and I want to pay you for it. Will a hundred dollars satisfy you for your afternoon's job?"

"Yes, sir, and more too; I don't ask anything for what I have done," I replied.

"Don't be too modest, my boy," added the major, placing a roll of bank bills in my hand.

"I am very much obliged to you, sir. I didn't ask or expect anything. I only came over here because I had to leave Centreport, and I did the work for the fun of it."

"Doubtless it was good fun; but you have done us a good turn, and I have not overpaid you. Now tell me about your difficulty with Wimpleton."

I told him the story about the events of the day. I think it quite likely the major thought he was encouraging a rebel; but he did not express any dissatisfaction with my conduct. On the contrary he praised my spirit, and declared that Middleport would be glad to take me up, if Centreport wished to cast me out. He then offered me a dollar a day to run the dummy; but I told him I could not accept it till I had consulted my father and mother, and it was arranged that I should see him the next day.

I then went to the shore, took my skiff, and rowed across the lake, feeling like a rich man.

CHAPTER XVII.

MOTHER'S ADVICE.

FOR the first time in my life I had some fears in regard to meeting my father. I dreaded the terrible infirmity which was beginning to develop itself anew in him. Under ordinary circumstances I should have been glad to see him; and with a hundred dollars in my pocket — the first money I had ever earned by my knowledge and skill — I should have been delighted to tell him the history of the day. I should have been sure of a proud and sympathetic listener in him as I detailed the means I had used to raise the dummy.

I feared two things — first, that he would be intoxicated; and second, that he would remember against me the deed I had done with the strange-looking bottle in the forenoon. In relation to the latter, I had come to see that the destruction of the whiskey was not the only or the greater cause of offence. By emptying the bottle, I had censured him, virtually, and made myself a judge of his condition and conduct. My father was a plucky man, in spite of his position as an employee of Colonel Wimpleton, and, right or wrong, would not suffer any one to be a censor upon his actions.

I feared that his anger would not go down with the sun; and I had an utter horror of any quarrel in the family. Besides, I had a great admiration of my father. I considered him one of the best and one of the most skilful men of his craft on the lake. I could not endure the thought of any coldness on his part or the feeling that I had suffered in his estimation. I knew he had been proud of me as a scholar, and especially proud of the reputation I had earned as a young engineer. My readers, therefore, will not be surprised when I say that my bosom bounded with emotion as I thought of meeting him after the occurrences of the day. If he was only sober, and in his right mind, all would be well with me.

I had heard in Middleport that the Ruoara, on

her down trip, had obtained an engineer at Hitaca; therefore I supposed my father had gone home. The storekeeper on the wharf had seen him; but I did not dare to ask whether he was intoxicated. Never before, I repeat, had I gone to my father's house with any doubts or misgivings. It was quite dark when I reached the mill wharf, and secured my skiff at its moorings. When I started from Middleport with a hundred dollars in my pocket, I felt like a rich man. During my silent pull across the lake I thought of our family trouble, and when I landed at Centreport I felt as though I had lost a hundred dollars, and that I was even poorer than usual.

With stealthy step I crept through the garden, fearful that I might encounter my father intoxicated. There was a light in the kitchen, and I stood on tiptoe, so that I could look in at the window. My father was not there. The supper table was waiting in the middle of the room, and my good mother sat at one corner of it, sewing, while my two sisters were reading near her. I opened the back door and went in, but not without the fear that I should be told my father was helpless in his bed.

"Why, Wolfert, where have you been?" asked my mother, rising as I entered. "I needn't ask you, for I have heard all about it."

"About what?"

"You have been over to Middleport, at work for the Toppleton boys."

"I know it."

"Why did you do it?"

"Why shouldn't I do it, mother?" I inquired, not a little astonished to find that she was inflamed by the rivalry between the two houses.

"Why shouldn't you do it! Because it will make trouble, Wolfert. When the boat brought over the news that you had raised the dummy, or whatever they call the thing, and that you were running it on the railroad over there, the people howled just as though you had set the town on fire. The Wimpleton boys say they will mob you, tar and feather you, and I don't know what not," said my poor mother, who appeared to be really suffering under this manifestation of popular indignation.

"It seems just as though I am bound to put my foot in it, whether I will or not. Do folks tell the rest of the story?" I inquired.

"The rest of what story?" asked my mother, opening her eyes.

"Do they say that I was hunted out of town like a wild beast?" I demanded, indignantly.

"Why, no; they didn't say anything of that kind. The girls came home just before dark, and said everybody was talking about you; that you had turned traitor."

"Perhaps I have, mother; but I don't care a fig for this three-cent quarrel between the two sides of the lake. I hope you won't turn against me, mother," I added, choking up with emotion, so that I could not speak.

"Turn against you! Why, no, Wolfert, I shall never turn against you. Who ever heard of such a thing?"

"You seem to blame me for what I have done," I replied, wiping away a truant tear, and struggling hard for utterance.

"I only said what you have done will make trouble. You know Colonel Wimpleton will not like it; and he will punish us all for your acts."

"I couldn't help it, mother. I was driven away."

" What do you mean by being driven away ? "

It occurred to me that my mother knew nothing of what had happened since Waddie had called to deliver the fictitious message from his father; and I told her the whole story.

" If I know my father, he would kick me if I should get down on my knees to Waddie Wimpleton. Be that as it may, I won't do it," I added.

" I don't want you to do it. If it has come to that, I think we had all better go to the poorhouse at once," said my mother, with more spirit than I remembered to have seen her exhibit before; and I felt then that she was on my side.

" We won't go to the poorhouse," I replied, taking the hundred dollars from my wallet. " I made that to-day."

My mother opened her eyes again, as she was in the habit of doing when astonished. Then she counted the money, and for an instant a smile overspread her pleasant face. To me it was the pleasantest face in all the world, and I had never before seen it saddened for so long a time as it had been that day.

"A hundred dollars!" exclaimed she, looking at me.

"Yes, mother; that is what Major Toppleton gave me for getting the dummy out of the water, and putting it on the track. It was a good job."

"The major is liberal; and I only wish he and the colonel would be friends again."

"I wish they would; but whether they are or not, I'm not going to fight the battle of either one of them. Now, mother, I want to make a clean breast of it. What you said to me after the colonel went away wasn't lost upon me. I was sorry I called Waddie a liar to his face, though all the world knows that he is one; and I was really sorry that I had said anything saucy to the colonel. When Waddie said he was going to lick me, I apologized to him; and I did to the colonel when I saw him. I think I did it handsomely, considering that they were going to lick me."

"I'm glad you did, Wolfert."

"It was like pulling out half a dozen of my teeth to do it, but I did it; and I was sincere in doing it, too. I won't go down on my knees to any one, and I won't confess a crime of which I'm not guilty;" and in my zeal I struck the table a blow with my fist which made all the dishes dance upon it.

"Do right, Wolfert, and pray to God for strength. He will help you, and all will be well in the end. Have you seen anything of your father?"

"I haven't seen him; but he came over on the Ruoara from the other side. I supposed he was at home," I replied.

"I haven't seen anything of him since he went out this morning," she added, looking very anxious.

I ate my supper, still discussing the exciting topic of the day. I felt better; for, if my mother was on my side, I could afford to have almost everybody else against me; and she was a Christian woman, who would rather have buried me than had me do any great wrong. Whatever my readers, old and young, may think of me, I feel bound to say that I had tried to do right. I had been goaded into the use of impudent speech by the intolerable tyranny of the magnate of Centreport; but I had apologized for it, and had been willing to make any reasonable reparation. My mother had taught me, as a child, to go down on my knees before God, but never to man.

I kissed my sisters, who were younger than I, and they went to bed about eight o'clock. My mother and I could now talk about the condition of my father, which neither of us was willing to do before them. We wondered what had become of him; but I was pretty sure that he was somewhere in Centreport. It was a new experience in our family to be waiting at night for him, for he always spent his evenings at home.

I told my mother of the offer which Major Toppleton had made me to run the dummy. For a boy of my age, and at a distance from the great city, the proposition was a liberal one, for my father only had sixty dollars a month. It is true I was to do a man's work for half wages; but no boy in that region could make half the money offered to me at that time.

"I don't see how you can take up with the offer," said my mother. "Colonel Wimpleton would not have anything to do with us if we did anything to help along the people on the other side."

"I don't know that I can accept it, but it is a great pity I cannot," I replied, moodily; for I should have been glad to run the dummy for nothing if the major was not willing to pay me.

"It is a pity; but only think how mad the colonel would be if you should go!"

"I don't know that he could be any madder than he is now. I am sick and disgusted with this stupid quarrel!"

"I'm sure he would discharge your father if he should let you go over to Middleport to work for the major. Those two men hate each other like evil spirits," replied my mother.

"Of course I don't want father to lose his situation; and if it comes to that, I suppose I must decline the offer."

"I think you must, Wolfert."

"I will, mother," I added, sorely aggrieved at the alternative. "I will not do anything to make a quarrel, though I think it is about time I should be earning something."

"Perhaps there will be a chance for you on this side; for I am sure the colonel will do something to get even with the major on that railroad. He will get up another railroad, a balloon, a flying machine, or something or other."

" He can't build any railroad on this side," I replied. " The country is so rough that it would cost him all he is worth. But if he did, he wouldn't give me anything to do upon it."

" Perhaps he " —

My mother's remark was interrupted by a noise in the garden; and, fearful that my poor father had come home in a helpless condition, I went out to ascertain the cause of it. It was not my father; but I heard sounds which indicated that several persons were running away from the house. I ran to the fence, and saw three boys hastening up the road towards the Institute. If I was not much mistaken, Waddie Wimpleton was one of them; and I concluded that he was still intent upon punishing me for calling him a liar.

As I was about to go into the house, I discovered another form in the darkness, walking down the road. I knew the step. It was my father. I was very thankful that he was able to walk, though I noticed that his step was a little unsteady.

CHAPTER XVIII.

WADDIE'S MISTAKE.

I HASTENED into the house, and told my mother that father was coming. She bestowed upon me a glance so full of anxiety that I comprehended the question she desired to ask, and I added that he walked tolerably well.

"Was it he that made the noise we heard?" she inquired.

"No; some of the students have been around here, and I think I saw Waddie," I replied.

"What do they want?"

"I don't know; but I suppose they wish to see me."

"Do be careful, Wolfert."

"I'm not afraid of them, mother. I think I can take care of myself in the face of the whole crowd."

My father came in at the back door, interrupting

the conversation. His step was unsteady and his movements uncertain. He stayed a long time in the entry putting away his hat, but at last he entered the kitchen. He made desperate struggles to conceal his condition; but he failed to do so. I could see my poor mother's bosom bounding with emotion as the days of evil came back to her from the past. There was a tear in her eye; but she spoke not a word of reproach. My father walked across the room to his accustomed chair, and dropped heavily into it.

"Wolf!" said he in a tone which was intended to be sharp, but which was very thick from the effects of the liquor.

"I am here, father," I replied, as little able to control my feelings as my mother.

"You have been a bad boy!" he added, fiercely. "You have disgraced your father!"

I thought not, but I did not deem it advisable to say so, or to utter a word that would irritate him.

"I used to think you were a smart boy; but now I think you are a fool," he continued, with an oath, which I had never before heard him use. "With a pistol in your hand you let Christy carry off all my money. I wouldn't say anything about that, but you came home, insulted and abused Colonel Wimp'ton and his son. You hadn't done your worst yet; so you went over to Middleport, and turned traitor to the friends that feed and clothe you. I know all about it!"

It was no use to talk about these things while he was in his present condition, and I held my peace.

"I've seen Colonel Wimp'ton, and he ztold me all about it," my father went on, rapping the table violently with his fist. "I won't have my boy behave zo. I'll lick him first."

"Why, father, Wolfert has not done anything bad," interposed my mother.

"I zsay he has!" replied my father furiously. "He'n Waddie blowed up the canal boat. Then Wolf denied it, and insulted his best friends. Then he went off and run that dummy."

"Don't say anything, mother," said I to her, in a low tone.

"What's that?" demanded my father, suspiciously.

"What did you say, Wolf? Do you mean to insult me, as you did Colonel Wimp'ton?"

But I will not follow this unpleasant scene any further in detail. It was evident that my father had seen the magnate of Centreport, and that the great man had won him over. He was stormy, violent, and suspicious. He was angry with me, and then with my mother for speaking a word in my defence. Finally he wept like a child, declaring that his family had turned against him; and, overwhelmed by this maudlin grief, he went upstairs and threw himself upon my bed. I think he intended to occupy the spare chamber on the other side of the entry, for he was so angry with my mother and me that he was intent upon getting away from us.

We decided that it would be best to let him alone. He lay sobbing on the bed for a time, and then dropped asleep. My mother went in, and, having assured herself that he was in a comfortable position, took away the lamp. She and I sat up till midnight, talking over the bitter prospect before us. In his cups my father was another man. My mother told me with tears in her eyes, that he had abused her when he used to drink before. In his intoxication he seemed to hate the family he loved so well when he was sober.

At midnight he was still sleeping off the effects of his debauch, and we retired, hoping for better things in the morning. I was so tired that I went to sleep very soon. I occupied the spare chamber on the second floor, while my mother's room was downstairs. I do not know how long I had slept, but I was awakened by a violent noise in the opposite side of the house, which seemed to come from the apartment where my father was. I was startled, and immediately leaped out of bed, lighted a lamp, and hastily put on my clothes. Hearing my father's voice in excited tones, I rushed to the room with the lamp in my hand. I feared that the liquor he had drank had in some manner affected his brain, and induced a delirium.

I opened the door. I saw my father standing over the prostrate form of Waddie Wimpleton. The window was wide open, and I heard voices outside, as of other boys effecting a hasty retreat. Waddie lay still upon the floor, and his face was covered with blood.

"What is the matter, father?" I asked, terrified at the strange sight which I beheld.

"Don't you see what the matter is?" replied my father; but he seemed to be very much confused.

"What has happened?"

"I hardly know," answered he, gazing at the form of Waddie.

My father had slept several hours, and he appeared to be quite sober.

"This is Waddie Wimpleton," said I, bending over the fallen youth.

"I see it is. I felt a hand upon me, and I started up from the bed. Some one caught hold of me, and I struck right and left, till I heard some one fall," answered my father, rubbing his eyes, as if to stimulate his bewildered senses. "I thought it was some one who had come to rob me, and I couldn't help believing it was Christy Holgate."

"What in the world is the matter?" cried my mother, who now came into the room, pale and trembling with terror.

I explained, as far as I could, the circumstances of the affair. My father said nothing, but went to the window and looked out.

"There is a ladder under the window," said he.

"But Waddie is not a robber," added my mother, kneeling on the floor at his side. "His face is cut, and he seems to be stunned."

My father and I lifted him up, and placed him on the bed. My mother went to work upon him, sending me down to assure my sisters that no harm could come to them. I brought up some water and the camphor bottle. On my return my father seemed to be quite like himself, and was assisting in the restoration of the injured boy.

"He isn't badly hurt, I think," said my mother. "One of his front teeth is knocked in, and the blood on his face comes from a mere scratch. What in the world was he doing here?"

"I understand it now," I replied. "Waddie and the other fellows were after me. I saw them around the house about eight o'clock."

"What do they want of you?" asked my father, whose head had been filled with the other side of the story.

"They were going to punish me, I suppose, for what I said to Waddie and his father, though I apologized to both of them for it."

"What is to be done with this boy?" interposed my mother, anxiously, as Waddie opened his eyes, and looked wildly around the room. "I think the doctor had better see him."

I went for the doctor, and came back with him, for he had just returned from a night visit to a distant patient, and his horse was harnessed at the door. When we arrived, Waddie was sitting up in the kitchen. The physician examined his head, and declared that he had sustained no injury that he could perceive. My father, who had been alarmed for the consequences of the blow he had struck, breathed easier after this announcement.

"I'm going home," said Waddie, rising from the chair, after the doctor had finished his examination. "I'll bet you haven't theen the latht of thith thcrape. I thall"—

The scion put his hand up to his mouth, and wondered why he could not speak without lisping. He had fully recovered his senses, under the vigorous treatment of my mother, and with them came back the evil spirit which controlled him.

"What were you doing in my house, Waddie?" asked my father.

"What wath I doing? I wath going to give Wolf fitth for being a traitor and calling me a liar. And I'll do it yet, if it coths me my life!" replied Waddie, vigorously, as he held one hand on his mouth.

"I didn't think you'd break into a man's house in the night," added my father.

"Wolf ith going to work on the other thide, and that'th the only time we could catch him. What did you hit me for?" demanded the scion, rubbing his sore head with his hand.

"I did not know it was you, Waddie," answered my father, meekly. "You came into my room in the dark, when I was asleep."

"It wathn't your room. It wath Wolf'th room. What were you doing in there?"

"It's my own house, and I have a right to occupy any room I please," said my father, with more spirit than before.

"You were boothy latht night and didn't know what you were about."

My father's brow contracted, and his lips were compressed. To be told that he was intoxicated galled him sorely. Waddie declared that he had struck him on purpose, and that he should suffer for it. The doctor then took him into his chaise, and conveyed him to his home. My father was not satisfied with the situation. He went to the pump, and drank a large mug of water. He walked up and down the kitchen in silence for a moment, and then said he must see Colonel Wimpleton at once. He went, and by going through the grove he could reach the house as soon as the doctor.

I did not see him again that night, and he did not come out of his room till eight o'clock the next morning. I was very anxious to know how he would regard me, after the hard words he had spoken the night before. I was also curious to learn what had passed at Colonel Wimpleton's during his visit. Our relations with the magnate were certainly very singular and perplexing. As nearly as I could judge, my father stood exactly in my own position in regard to him. Neither of us had intended to insult or injure the great man or his son, but both had incurred his displeasure; for it would be impossible for the colonel to forgive the unwitting blow my father had struck.

"Wolf," said my father, after he had eaten his breakfast, "your mother tells me you have an offer on the other side."

"Yes, sir."

"You may accept it, and go to work to-day, if you wish."

"I should be very glad to do so," I replied. "Did you have any trouble with Colonel Wimpleton?"

"I did. He discharged me, and ordered me out of his house," he answered, gloomily.

Of one thing I was sure — my father was not angry with me.

CHAPTER XIX.

RICH MEN'S QUARRELS.

MY father was himself again. He was clothed in his right mind once more. He even appeared to have forgotten that I had emptied the bottle the day before, and treated me as kindly as though nothing had occurred to mar the unity which had always subsisted between us. My mother seemed to be quite happy, too; and, while I was at work in the garden, she told me she had talked till daylight with him, after his return from Colonel Wimpleton's. He had bitterly bewailed his error, and solemnly promised not to taste another drop of liquor. He was conscious that he had lost his twenty-four hundred dollars by getting intoxicated, and he had very little hope of ever seeing it again.

More than this, my mother had explained my conduct to him, and he was satisfied with it. The

night visit of Waddie, and the colonel's unreasonable harshness to him, had probably done more to
convince him than any words of my mother. He
had lost his situation, and had been treated with
gross injustice, for the great man would not accept
his explanation of the blow he had given his son.

"Wolf," said my father, after he had granted me
permission to accept Major Toppleton's offer, "I am
afraid we shall soon be in trouble all round."

"I hope not."

"If I had the money to pay off the mortgage
on the house, I should not care so much. As it
is, I may lose even the thousand dollars I have paid
on it. The colonel will foreclose on me at once,
and people here will not dare to bid when it is put
up at auction, if he tells them not to do so."

"I heard you say you had an offer of thirty-five
hundred dollars for the place."

"So I had; Bingham offered that for it."

"I would go to him, and take the offer at once."

"What, sell the place?"

"Yes; you can pay off the mortgage, and then
have fifteen hundred left."

"That's a good idea," replied my father. "But I don't know that Bingham will give thirty-five hundred now."

"I would try him, at any rate. I think we had better move out of Centreport."

"Perhaps it would be as well, after what has happened," said he, in deep thought. "I will see what can be done."

My father hastened to the village to see Bingham, and soon after I pulled across the lake to report for duty to Major Toppleton. I was shown into his elegant library; but I found the magnate of Middleport in violent wrath.

"I have called, sir, to say that I will accept the offer you were so kind as to make to me yesterday," I began, with the utmost deference.

"Very well, boy. I am a man of honor, which cannot be said of every man who lives on the other side of the lake," — by which, of course, he meant Colonel Wimpleton, — "and I will keep my agreement; but if the business were to be done over again, I wouldn't have anything to do with a person from Centreport."

"I'm sorry you think so hard of us, sir," I ventured to reply. "I will do the very best I can for you; and I hope we shall not live in Centreport much longer."

"Well, I don't know that I need to blame you for what Wimpleton does. He is a mean man, and his soul is smaller than a mosquito's. This morning the old rascal sent his agent over here to offer the engineer of my flour mills twenty dollars a month more than he is getting now. The villain was paid up to last night, and left without giving me any notice, and my mills are all stopped."

Major Toppleton walked the library in a violent rage, and I waited for further developments before I dared to speak.

"He hired my engineer away from me, I'm told, because I employed you," added the magnate, pausing before me.

"I'm very sorry I made any trouble," I answered, diffidently.

"You didn't make it. I only wonder how Wimpleton was my friend for so many years. He omits no opportunity to stab me when he gets a chance.

I suppose he is gloating over it now because no smoke rises from my mills."

" Do you want an engineer, sir? " I had the audacity to ask at this opportune moment.

" Of course I do. Wimpleton sent over for mine solely to vex me, and I would give a thousand dollars to be even with him this moment."

" I can run the engine of your mills," I replied.

" You? "

" Yes, sir; I have run the Centreport mills for a week at a time."

" But I want you on the dummy."

" I will bring you an engineer, then, in an hour. What wages will you give, sir? "

" I will give the same that Wimpleton pays the man he stole from me — eighty dollars a month, and engage him for a year."

" I will have him here in one hour, sir."

" But who is he? "

" My father, sir."

" Oh, ho ! "

" Colonel Wimpleton discharged him before daylight this morning."

14

"Then I am to take a man whom Wimpleton has discharged, and pay him twenty dollars more than he was having before."

"He discharged my father in order to punish him," I replied; and then I told him the sequel to the story I had related the day before.

"Very good! Excellent! I will help Wimpleton punish your father by giving him eighty dollars a month, which is twenty dollars more than any engineer ought to have. Go for him at once."

I never pulled across the lake so quickly before as I did then. I found my father at home; he had just returned from his visit to Bingham.

"Back so soon, Wolf?" said he; and he looked quite sad.

"Yes, sir. Did you see Bingham?"

"I did; but it's too late. He has heard of the quarrel, and won't buy the house at any price. It will go hard with me, I'm afraid."

"Never mind, father. It will come out right in the end, I know."

"What did you come back for?"

"Major Toppleton wants you, and will engage you

for a year, at eighty dollars a month," I replied, with proper enthusiasm.

" Eighty dollars ! "

I explained what Colonel Wimpleton had done, and what Major Toppleton wished to do.

" He wants you right off, this minute," I added.

" I'm all ready."

" When rich men quarrel, poor men ought to profit by it, if they can do so honestly," I suggested.

" The colonel will be the maddest man this side of the north pole, when he hears of my good fortune," said my father.

" I dare say he will, for it appears that he has only discharged you to open the way to a much better position."

" Exactly so ! " exclaimed my father, delighted with the situation. " If rich men will be fools, we cannot help it, as you say, Wolf."

My father took the bundle of old clothes he had just brought from the mill ; and we went down to the wharf, where we embarked in the skiff for the other side of the lake.

" If you could only sell the place, father, we

might move over to Middleport at once," said I, pulling with all my might at the oars.

"I don't think I can do it. By this time everybody knows that the colonel has quarrelled with me, and no one will run the risk of offending him by buying it," replied my father. "I hope Mortimer will catch Christy, and get back part of my money, if not the whole of it."

We landed in Middleport, and hastened to the mansion of the major. He was ever so much better humored than when I had called upon him before. He had evidently considered the nature of the victory he had won over his powerful rival, for he had certainly cheated the colonel out of his revenge upon my father, and practically nullified his punishment. He appeared to be duly comforted.

"I am glad to see you, Mr. Penniman," said he, graciously, as my father bowed low to him.

"I am very grateful to you for your kind offer, sir, and I accept it thankfully," replied my father.

"I wish to see the smoke rising from the chimney of the mill at once," added the major, briskly. "I want Wimpleton to understand that he can't shut me up. Go to the mill, and get up steam as fast as you can; and the more smoke you make, the better, for that will be my sign of triumph."

" I'll fire up at once," replied my father, leaving the room, and hastening to his work.

Young and inexperienced as I was, I could not help feeling sad at this exhibition of malignity on the part of the rich man of Middleport. The colonel had taken the opportunity afforded by the dismissal of my father to strike his rival in a tender place. It was mean; but such was the character of the dealings between them, when they had any. The major rubbed his hands with delight, and paced the library under the exhilaration of the moment. It was a pity that these men, with such vast means of doing good within their grasp, should quarrel with each other, and debase and demoralize a whole neighborhood by their actions.

" Well, Mr. Penniman, I suppose you are ready to go to work," said the major, pausing before me after a time.

Mr. Penniman! I felt an inch taller to have a handle applied to my name by such a magnificent man.

" Yes, sir; I am waiting for orders."

" I suppose you think that dummy isn't much of an engine," he added, with a very pleasant smile upon his face.

" I think it works very well, sir."

" I dare say you do; but I want to say, a thing like that is not the height of our ambition," he continued, rubbing his hands under the influence of some undeveloped idea.

" I'm sure I shouldn't wish for anything better than the dummy."

" It answers very well to begin with; but I have a regular locomotive and two cars in process of building, and I shall have them on the track this fall."

" Is it a big locomotive?" I asked, curiously.

" No, it's a small one; and it will be the prettiest plaything you ever saw. I'm determined that the Toppleton Institute shall be the most popular one in the country."

" I suppose Colonel Wimpleton will do something to offset this movement on your part," I suggested.

" What can he do?" asked the major, anxiously. " Have you heard of anything?"

"No, sir. I only know they feel very bad about the Lake Shore Railroad over there."

"They will feel worse before we get through with it," replied the magnate, shaking his head. "What can they do? They can't build a railroad, the country is so rough. We can keep ahead of them now. But I want that dummy in motion. You must run it every half hour for the rest of the day between Middleport and Spangleport. Carry everybody who wishes to ride. I want the Centreport people to see it, and to know that we are alive on this side."

"Will the students be with me?" I inquired.

"This afternoon, when they are dismissed from the school-room, they will be. I will send you a conductor. Let me see; Higgins is too sick to study, and just sick enough to play. He shall run with you. Now keep her going, as though you meant business."

"I will, sir; I will put her through by daylight," I replied, as I left the library.

CHAPTER XX.

THE BEAUTIFUL PASSENGER.

I FOUND the dummy just as I had left it on the preceding day. I kindled a fire in the furnace, rubbed down the machinery, filled up the water tank, and took on a supply of coal, which was the kind of fuel intended to be used under the boiler. I assure my sympathetic reader that I felt a real pleasure in the discharge of these duties, and in the consciousness that I was actually the master of the machine. Though my taste was rather inclined towards the engine of a steamer, I was more than satisfied with my present position, and deemed myself the luckiest dog in the world.

Higgins, the invalid student, who was to officiate as conductor, stood by and watched all my movements with the most intense interest. He looked like a clever fellow, and I proceeded to make friends with him in due form, by declaring that I was sorry he was sick.

"I'm not sorry," said he with a grin. "I'm rather glad I'm sick. In fact, I'm not very sick."

"Well, I thought you were; the major said so; at least he said you were too sick to study, and just sick enough to play."

"Did he say that?"

"He did."

"Well, he knows a thing or two," laughed Higgins. "My mother thinks it makes my head ache to study; and in fact it does when the lessons are hard."

"I dare say. Are they hard to-day?" I asked.

"Not so very hard; but, to tell the truth, I thought there was to be some fun going on here and I wanted to be on hand. My mother wrote to the principal that she did not wish me to study very hard, for something ailed my head."

"I'm afraid the jar of the dummy will hurt your head," I suggested.

"Oh, no, it won't," protested the candid Higgins. "It feels better now than it did this morning; in fact, it always feels better after school begins."

"But I'm really afraid it will injure you to ride on the dummy, with all the excitement of the highly responsible position of conductor," I added, gravely. "I think I had better mention the matter to Major Toppleton when I see him."

"Oh, no; don't do that," pleaded Higgins, plaintively. "Between you and me and the smoke-stack of the dummy, I am as well as you are."

"Precisely so; and I think the major understands your malady, if the principal does not."

"Don't say a word this time, and I won't 'soger' any more."

"It's none of my business, Higgins, but you are sawing off your own nose, and playing the trick upon yourself. I would be a man and face the music like one, if I were you."

"I will face the music if you won't say anything."

"All ready, Mr. Conductor!" I shouted, when I had steam enough.

"All aboard!" yelled Higgins, rather glad to change the subject when he found that I did not appreciate his deception.

I ran the dummy out of the house, and stopped

her near the head of the steamboat wharf. The car was still so great a novelty that many people gathered around to examine it. The cushions were now well dried, and though the cloth had suffered somewhat from the effects of the bath, it looked very nice inside of her.

"Have you a watch, Higgins?" I asked of the gentlemanly conductor.

"Yes," replied he, producing a small gold one.

"We will leave Middleport on the hour, and Spangleport on the half hour," I added. "I wish I had a watch."

"Why don't you have one?"

"I'm not a rich man's son, and I can't afford to have such playthings. But I suppose I must get one, if I run on this dummy."

"I'll lend you mine for to-day, Wolf."

"Thank you. I want to time the running, so as to know where we are," I answered, taking the watch, and attaching the chain to my vest. "It is nearly twelve o'clock, and we will start soon."

"All aboard for Spangleport!" screamed Higgins,

as though the announcement was intended for the people on the other side of the lake.

"Folks will understand that nothing ails your lungs, Higgins, whatever is the matter with your head," I added, gently, to the zealous conductor. "I wouldn't yell so. Boys always make fools of themselves by hallooing when there isn't the least need of it."

Higgins, in a milder tone, invited the ladies and gentlemen who were inspecting the car to step in and make the excursion to Spangleport, promising that they should return in just fifty minutes. Quite a number of them accepted the invitation; and I was about to start, when I saw a very beautiful young lady hastening towards us. She was elegantly dressed, and her movements were as graceful as those of a fawn. The "gentlemanly conductor" rang the bell for the engine to start, and the young lady, hearing it, made a motion with her sunshade for us to wait for her. I was too happy to find she was to be a passenger in the car to start without her, in spite of my laudable ambition to be "on time."

The moment Higgins saw her, he jumped off the platform, took off his cap, bowed and scraped like a French dancing-master, and helped her up the steps. There was a glass window in the partition between the engine-room and the passenger compartment, for which at that moment I felt extremely grateful to the builder, for it enabled me to obtain an occasional glance at the beautiful young lady. I beg leave to say that this unwonted enthusiasm on my part was as surprising to myself as it will be to my readers, for I had hardly ever looked at any person of the feminine persuasion before, except my mother and sisters. I had certainly never seen any lady who attracted me so strongly, or for whom I felt so great an admiration. She was not more than fifteen or sixteen years of age; but she wore a long dress, and had a mature bearing.

Higgins conducted her to a seat, and she took possession of it as gracefully as though she had been schooled in the polite art for a whole lifetime. I could not help gazing at her, and I envied Higgins the rapture of being permitted to speak to her. She looked around, and bowed to several persons in the car, with the sweetest smile that ever lighted up a young lady's face. I was wholly absorbed in gazing at her, and actually forgot that I was the young engineer of the Lake Shore Railroad, till the sharp snap of the bell brought me to my senses, and assured me that Higgins was not so fascinated as I was.

I was a minute behind time, and I let on the steam to make it up. I was obliged to turn my back on the beautiful being in the car, and look out for " breakers ahead " through the door and windows in the end of the engine-room; but I had the pleasing satisfaction of thinking that in running backwards from Spangleport I should face the other way.

What a fool I was ! Of course I was. A young man always has a time to be a fool, just as he has to take the measles, though he seldom has it so young as I did. I did not know who the young lady was, and I did not crave any other privilege than that of simply looking at her, just as I should at a pretty picture. If she had fallen overboard, I should certainly have jumped in after her. If she had been in the claws of a lion, I should certainly have smitten the lion. If she had been in the upper story of a house on fire, I should certainly have run the risk of being singed for her sake. But she did not fall overboard, or into the claws of a lion, and she was not in a burning house ; and, provoking as it was, I could not do anything for her, except turn my back to her, — and I was not sure that this was not the most agreeable service I could render her, — and run the dummy at its highest speed.

I could not help seeing the beautiful young lady even through the back of my head ; and I am sorry to say that I forgot to look at my watch, when we passed Ruggles's barn and the Grass Brook bridge, as I had intended ; and at a quarter past twelve the dummy sizzled into Spangleport, shivering like an over-driven horse. I had the self-possession, however, to stop her when she got there ; but I have since wondered that, under the circumstances, I did not run her into the lake, or over the hill to Grass Springs. I had made the distance in just fourteen minutes.

The passengers got out of the car, and for a time I lost sight of the elegant young lady. Higgins came round to me, and declared that we had made a " bully trip." I was entirely of his opinion ; but I was not willing to confess that a certain absent-mindedness had induced me to run the machine so as to gain five minutes, and make up one. The conductor left me, and I fancied that he had gone to find the interesting person who had fascinated me, and with whom he seemed to be acquainted.

" Will you allow me to get in there and see the machinery?" said a silvery voice, while I was rubbing up the works.

I turned, and my face felt as though all the steam in the boiler had been discharged upon it when I discovered that the speaker was no other than the bewitching being who was uppermost in my thoughts.

"Certainly," I replied, leaping to the ground, and endeavoring to imitate the polite gyrations of the gentlemanly conductor.

"'Thank you, Mr. Wolf," added she, with the sweetest of smiles.

Mr. Wolf ! Involuntarily my head went up, and I felt prouder of the handle to my name then when the mighty major himself had applied it.

"I'm afraid you will find the engine-room a very dirty and greasy place," I had the courage to suggest, flustered as I was by having the beautiful girl speak to me — actually speak to me!

"Oh, never mind! I have on my old clothes."

If these were her old clothes, I wondered what her best were.

"I suppose you don't know me, Mr. Wolf; but I have heard a great deal about the young engineer, and I assure you I am delighted to see you," she added, with a kind of roguish look, which made me feel just as though I was "going up." "I am Grace Toppleton."

The daughter of the major! I had heard what a pretty, gentle, amiable girl she was, and I was positively sure that the reports did not belie her.

"I have often heard of you, though I never had the pleasure of seeing you before," I replied, as gallantly as my flustered state of mind would permit.

Still imitating the gentlemanly conductor, I took her gloved hand, and attempted to help her up the high step of the engine-room. I felt, at this particular moment, just as though I was in the seventh

15

heaven. As the elegant young lady was about to step up, a rude grasp was laid on my shoulder; so rude that Miss Grace lost her foothold on the step, and was thrown back upon the ground.

Turning round, I discovered that my rough assailant was Captain Synders, the constable of Centreport. He was attended by Colonel Wimpleton and the skipper of the canal boat which had been blown up. To my astonishment, Miss Grace leaped upon the dummy without my help, and I was held back by the savage grasp of the officer. My blissful dream had suddenly been disturbed, and I was mad. The envious Centreporters had chosen the moment of my greatest joy to pounce upon me.

THE VISITORS FOR CENTREPORT. Page 226.

CHAPTER XXI.

SOME TALK WITH COLONEL WIMPLETON.

I WAS very intent upon explaining to Miss Grace Toppleton the mysteries of the dummy engine, and I was not pleased to have the agreeable interview broken off. I was vexed, annoyed, and disconcerted. The beautiful young lady looked at me, and I thought I could see the indications of sympathy upon her face.

"If you will excuse me a moment, Miss Toppleton, I will show you the engine," I said to her, with all the politeness of which my nature was capable.

"I guess not," added Captain Synders, with a coarse grin, as though he had evil intentions in regard to me.

"If you will let me, Mr. Wolf, I want to ride back in the engine-room, and see the machinery work," replied she, in her silvery tones.

"I guess not," repeated Captain Synders; and I turned my attention from her to him.

I could not conceive why Colonel Wimpleton and his odious associate had chosen to come down upon me at Spangleport, rather than Middleport, unless it was because their appearance would make less excitement. The boat in which they had come lay at the wharf, and they must have started long before the dummy left Middleport. Possibly they expected to interrupt the trips of the engine, and have it left five miles from its headquarters without an engineer.

Colonel Wimpleton had with him Captain Synders, the constable. It had not yet occurred to me that I should actually be arrested, and held to answer for the destruction of the honest skipper's canal boat, though the appearance of the officer had suggested the idea to me. They could not arrest me without including Waddie in the warrant, for he had confessed his agency in the mischief. I did not know of any way by which I could be punished without involving the scion of the great house on the other side.

"What do you wish with me?" I asked, in a

very ill-natured tone; for I beg to remind the reader that I am human, and that Miss Toppleton occupied the engine-room of the car.

Captain Synders glanced at the colonel, as though he expected him to do the talking, and that distinguished gentleman looked down upon me with unutterable severity. The honest skipper did not appear to have much sympathy with his companions, and looked very pleasant for a man who had experienced so heavy a loss as that of his canal boat.

" Wolf ! " said the colonel, in stern and lofty accents.

" Sir ! " I replied, with a dignity becoming the engineer of the Lake Shore Railroad.

" We have been looking for you," he added, glancing at the constable, as if to direct my attention to him.

" You have been lucky enough to find me, sir. I wish to say, sir, that the car starts for Middleport at half-past twelve, and therefore I have only ten minutes to spare," I replied, consulting Higgins's gold watch, the appearance of which, I think, produced a sensation in the minds of my visitors.

"Humph! I think you will wait my pleasure."

"That will depend somewhat upon the length of time your pleasure demands my presence. Will you please to tell me what you want of me?"

"Where is your father, Wolf?"

"At Middleport, sir."

"What is he doing there?"

"He is at work, sir."

Colonel Wimpleton looked as though he wanted to swear; for I am sorry to say this influential man sometimes indulged in the wicked habit of using profane language. It did not seem quite proper that the menial, whom he had discharged as a punishment, should find work so soon.

"What is he doing?" demanded the magnate of Centreport, biting his lips to conceal his vexation.

"You were so kind as to make an opening for him, sir, by hiring away Major Toppleton's engineer, and my father has taken his place, at the same wages — eighty dollars a month — as you pay your new engineer."

The great man stamped his foot with rage, and uttered an expression with which I cannot soil my paper. As wicked, tyrannical, overbearing men often do, he had overreached himself in his anxiety to strike my father. If it was unchristian for me to rejoice in his discomfiture, I could not help it, and I did so most heartily.

"I have been to see him about your conduct," continued the colonel, when his wrath would let him speak again. "I want to know what he is going to do about paying his share of the loss of the canal boat which you and Waddie blew up?"

"I can speak for him, sir, if that is all you want. He is not going to pay the first cent of it," I replied.

"Here is the captain of the boat, and he wants to know what you are going to do about it," added the colonel, trying to enjoy the confusion which he thought I ought to feel in view of such a demand.

"Yes, I want to know who is going to pay for the mischief," said the honest skipper; but as he already knew, he did not put much heart into the words, and actually chuckled as he uttered them.

"Captain," I continued, turning to the master of the canal boat, "I say to you, as I have said to others, that I had nothing whatever to do with blowing up your boat, and I did not know anything about it till the explosion took place. That is all I have to say."

"I don't know anything about it," replied the skipper.

"I do," interposed the colonel. "He has confessed that he had hold of the string when the boat blew up."

I took the trouble to explain to the honest skipper that Waddie had asked me to pull in his kite line; that I had picked it up, but, fearing some trick, had done nothing with it; and that Waddie had pulled the string himself.

"All aboard for Middleport!" shouted Higgins, as moderately this time as a gentlemanly conductor should speak.

"My time is nearly up, sir," I added to the colonel. "If you have any further business with me, please to state it as quickly as possible."

"You must go over to Centreport with me, and arrange this business," replied the magnate, gruffly.

"No, sir; I cannot do that."

"Then Captain Synders must arrest you."

"Very well, sir; let him do so. I am willing to go to jail and stand trial on the blowing up. Have you made a complaint against me?" I asked of the honest skipper.

He was too candid to tell a lie, and he made me no answer.

"Have you a warrant for my arrest?" I demanded of Captain Synders.

"I can take you without a warrant," growled the constable.

"Do so, then. If you wish to arrest me, I will submit."

My friends may think I was putting a very bold face upon the matter, but I candidly admit that I should have been glad to have the charge against me investigated; though I was very certain no steps would be taken in that direction. It is possible Colonel Wimpleton believed that I had been concerned with his hopeful in the blowing up of the canal boat; yet the guilt of his son was settled, and, if convicted, some stupid judge might sentence us both to the penitentiary, for the case would have to go to the shire town of the county, out of the reach of the great man's influence, for trial.

My father had told me that, at the interview with the colonel in the night, the latter had threatened him with prosecution for abusing his son; but when my father suggested that Waddie had broken into his house in the night time, it was plain enough that the young gentleman was liable to a turn in the state prison. Waddie's crimes and mistakes continually stood in the way of his taking his revenge. I considered myself fully protected in the same manner.

"Captain Synders, if you are going to arrest me, please to do it at once," I added, as the lady passengers began to get into the car, and some of the gentlemen came up to the spot where I stood.

"What's the row?" asked Higgins.

"These gentlemen from the other side talk of taking me up for the mischief to that canal boat. If they do so, Higgins, I want you to go to my father, and tell him about it. If I mistake not, Waddie Wimpleton will be arrested before night for breaking into our house."

"I'll do it!" exclaimed the enthusiastic conductor.

"Arrest Waddie!" ejaculated the colonel, gnashing his teeth with rage.

It was mortifying to the great man to find that he had come to the end of his rope; that even his power to annoy and persecute his inferiors had a limit.

"All aboard!" repeated Higgins.

"If you are going to arrest me, Captain Synders, now is your time," I added.

The people who had gathered around us began to laugh and enjoy the scene, and, being mostly Middleporters, they had no particular sympathy for the colonel.

"Wolf, we shall meet again," said the great man, sullenly, as he turned upon his heel, and, followed by his companions, walked rapidly down to the wharf, where his boat lay.

Even while I knew his power, and felt that he could annoy our family, and perhaps ruin us, I was quite ready to meet him again. Waddie's indiscretions stood between me and his wrath for the present, but his time might come. I leaped into the engine-room of the dummy, where Miss Toppleton had stood listening to our conversation.

" Mr. Wolf, I think you are real smart," said she, with a sweet smile of approbation.

" I thank you, Miss Toppleton, for your good opinion. Colonel Wimpleton is very hard upon me just now."

" I heard father tell about it. I think that Colonel Wimpleton is a real wicked man; and I only wonder that he and father were good friends for so many years."

" I am all ready to start now," I added. " I wish I had better accommodations for you."

" Oh, this is very nice ! " exclaimed she.

I opened the valve, and let on the steam.

" What did you do then ? " she asked, pointing to the handle of the valve.

" I let on the steam ; " and then I gave her a full description of the engine, which was hardly finished when we came in sight of Middleport.

I found it a delightful task to expatiate on my favorite theme to such a beautiful and interested listener, and I pointed out the cylinder wherein the piston worked, the connecting rod which moved the crank, and showed her how the valves which admitted the steam to the cylinder were worked. I flattered myself, after the lesson I had given her, that she was almost competent to run the dummy herself.

"I think it is real nice to ride in here, and see the machinery move," said she.

"So do I; and I enjoy it very much; more just now, I fear, than I ever shall again."

"Why so?" she asked, innocently.

I was not quite bold enough to explain the principal reason, and so I replied that it was a new thing to me.

"I hope you will let me ride with you again, some time," she added.

"With the greatest pleasure," I replied. "Whenever you please."

We ran into Middleport, and Miss Toppleton thanked me very prettily for my kindness in showing her about the engine; and I really wished I had it to do over again. By this time the students were turned out of school, and all of them gathered around the dummy, anxious to begin the afternoon's fun. I had brought over my dinner, and I ate it before the next trip. At one o'clock I was ready to start for Spangleport again.

CHAPTER XXII.

THE CONSTRUCTION TRAIN.

I HAVE been so busy with the history of our family affairs, and the incidents which sent me over to Middleport, that I have not had much to say about the Lake Shore Railroad; but before I have done with the subject, I shall fully describe the road, and explain the operations of the company. Only a small portion of the line had yet been built, and the dummy was but a temporary substitute for more complete rolling stock. Major Toppleton intended to have a charter for the road, to be obtained at the next session of the legislature, and to continue it to Ucayga. Although it was at the present time a mere plaything for the students, it was designed to be a useful institution, and to build up Middleport immensely in the end.

Just as I was about to start on the one o'clock

trip, Major Toppleton presented himself. The car was filled with students, though a number of ladies and gentlemen had come down to the station to have a ride in the dummy. The major immediately ordered the boys to evacuate the premises, which they did with some grumblings, amounting almost to rebellion. The persons waiting were invited to get in, and I started for Spangleport with a less noisy crowd than I had anticipated. As we went off, I heard the major call the students together, and I concluded that he had some definite plan to carry out.

On my return, I found the boys had loaded up the two platform cars with rails and sleepers, and they were attached to the dummy as soon as she arrived. Several mechanics were standing by, and it was evident that a piece of work was to be done that day, instead of play.

" Now, Wolf, we will run a construction train on this trip," said Major Toppleton, as he took his place at my side on the dummy, and directed the students and the mechanics to load themselves into the passenger apartment and on the cars.

" I think we need a little more construction at Spangleport, sir," I suggested.

" Why, what's the matter?"

" I don't like to run backwards, sir, on the down trips."

" But a turn-table will cost too much for the short time we shall make Spangleport a terminus. We will build one at Grass Springs, for that will be as far as we shall run the road this season."

" We need not build a turn-table, sir," I added. " We can turn the dummy on switches."

" How is that?" inquired the major.

" It will take three switches to turn her. First run a track round a curve to the right, until it comes to a right angle with the main line. Then run another track on the reverse curve till it strikes the main line again, a few rods from the point where the first track leaves it."

" I don't understand it."

" I will explain it when we stop, sir. It will not take long to lay it down, and when it is no longer wanted it can be taken up, and put down in another place."

16

At Spangleport, where we stopped, I made a diagram on a piece of paper, to illustrate my plan; and
here is a copy of my drawing. The perpendicular

lines are the main track. The dummy was to be
switched off at the lowest part of the diagram, and
run on the curve till it had passed a switch on the
right.   Then it was to be switched on the upper
curve, and run back till it passed the switch on the
main line, which being shifted, the car having been
turned entirely round, it runs back on the perpendicular lines between the curves.

Major Toppleton was satisfied with the scheme,
directed that the switches should be brought up,
and the work was commenced at once by the mechanics.   All the boys but two were employed in
laying down more track; but I am sorry to say
they grumbled fiercely, for they wanted to have
some fun with the dummy. Higgins was still to

serve as conductor, and the other student who had been excepted from hard labor was one of the regularly appointed engineers of the road. His name was Faxon. He had some taste for mechanics, and had distinguished himself in school by making a fine diagram of the steam-engine on the blackboard. He was to run with me on the dummy, and learn to manage the engine. I was directed to post him up, as well as I could, and to permit him to take an active part in running the machine.

I was not particularly pleased with the idea of an apprentice in the engine-room with me, for if the fellow had any " gumption " he would soon be able to take my place, and I might be discharged whenever it was convenient. But a second thought assured me that my fears were mean and unworthy; that I could never succeed in making myself useful by keeping others in ignorance. The students were sent to the Institute to learn, and the railroad was a part of their means of instruction. I had no right to be selfish.

We ran down to the wharf in Spangleport, for the road was built half a mile beyond the village, when Higgins shouted, "All aboard for Middle-port!" We had quite a crowd of Spangleporters as passengers, and we ran our trips regularly till five o'clock, to the great gratification of the people of both places, when the gentlemanly conductor declined to receive any more who expected to return, as the half-past five car up would be a construction train. Mr. Higgins talked very glibly and professionally by this time, and imitated all the gentlemanly conductors he had ever seen.

Faxon was a very good fellow, though he cherished a bitter antipathy against the Wimpletonians, and everything connected with them. He was an ardent admirer of Major Toppleton, and particularly of Major Toppleton's eldest daughter, for which I did not like him any the less, strange as it may appear after the developments of the last chapter.

"I'll tell you what it is, Wolf," said he, as we were running up the last trip, "this thing won't go down with the fellows."

"What?"

"All the fellows are mad because they had to work this afternoon."

"I thought they considered it fun to build the road."

"They did before the dummy came; but now they want the fun of the thing. They are all rich men's sons, and they won't stand it to work like Irish laborers. I hope there won't be any row."

"Of course Major Toppleton knows what he is about."

"The students don't growl before him. They do it to the teachers, who dare not say their souls are their own."

"But the major told me the boys enjoyed the fun, and insisted upon building the road themselves when he wanted to employ laborers for the purpose."

"That's played out. I heard some of the fellows say they would not work another day."

"Some one ought to tell the major about this. He don't want them to work if they don't like it," I suggested.

"It was fine fun when we first began to dig, and lay rails, but we have all got about enough of it."

"I will speak to the major about it."

"Don't say anything to-day," interposed Faxon. "The students are vexed because they were not allowed to have a good time this afternoon; but the major is going to have a great picnic at Sandy Shore next week, and he is in a hurry to have the road built to that point — two miles beyond Spangleport."

"There is only one mile more to build, and if the fellows stick to it they will get it done."

"But they say they won't work another day," replied Faxon.

Middleport was not paradise any more than Centreport. Boys were just as foolish and just as willing to get into a scrape, on one side as the other. The Toppletonians had insisted upon doing the work of building the road, and then purposed to rebel because they were required to do it. I had heard of the grand picnic which was to take place on the occasion of the birthday of Miss Grace Toppleton. The grove by the Sandy Shore could be reached most conveniently by the railroad, and the major's anxiety to have the rails laid to that point had induced him to drive the work, instead of giving the students a chance to have a good time with the dummy, as they had desired to do while it was a new thing.

We ran into the engine-house, and some of the boys forced their way into my quarters, in spite of my protest. I saw a couple of them studying the machinery with deep interest. They asked me some questions; and supposing they were only gratifying a reasonable curiosity, I gave them all the information they needed, telling them just how to manage the engine.

"Pooh! I can do that as well as anybody," said Briscoe, as he jumped down.

"Of course you can," replied one of his companions.

"Don't you think I could run her, Wolf?" asked Briscoe. "I am one of the engineers of the road, and I ought to know how."

"Probably you could after you had had some experience."

They went away, and I wondered what they were thinking about. It did not much matter, however, for I was satisfied that the major would not permit them to run the engine till they had become thoroughly competent to do so. I put out the fires in the dummy, cleaned the machinery, and left her in readiness for use the next morning. I then went to the mills; and, as my father had finished his day's work, we walked down to the wharf where my skiff lay. On the way I told him about my interview with Colonel Wimpleton, and we both enjoyed the great man's confusion when he learned in what manner he had punished my father.

"He will not arrest you, Wolf; you may depend upon that," said my father. "As the case now stands, we have the weather-gauge on him, except in the matter of the mortgage. I am afraid I shall lose all I have in the house. Mortimer has got back, but he hasn't seen or heard of Christy."

"He may turn up yet."

"He may, but I don't depend much upon it. I have tried a little here in Middleport to raise the money to pay off the mortgage; but people here will not lend anything on real estate on the other side of the lake."

" Perhaps Major Toppleton will help you out," I suggested.

" I don't like to say anything to him about it. He has done well by me, and I won't ride a free horse to death; besides, I don't want to be in the power of either one of these rich men. I have had trouble enough on the other side."

I pulled across the lake, and we went into the house. My mother looked anxiously at my father as he entered, and then at me. I smiled, and she understood me. Father had not drank a drop, and she was happy. We never relished our supper any better than we did that night, and I went to bed early, not a little surprised that we heard nothing, during the evening, of Colonel Wimpleton and his son.

The dummy was to make her first trip at eight o'clock, and I left the house at half-past six, with my father, to cross the lake. When we reached the wharf, I was utterly confounded to see the dummy streaking it at the rate of twenty miles an hour along the opposite shore of the lake. Something was wrong, for there was no one on the other side who knew how to run the machine, unless it was Faxon, and I was afraid the discontented Toppletonians were in mischief. We embarked in the skiff, and I pulled over as quickly as I had done the day before.

CHAPTER XXIII.

OFF THE TRACK.

THE appearance of the dummy, going at full speed, filled me with anxiety. I was sure that something was wrong, for I knew that Major Toppleton was not stirring at that hour in the morning, and that he could not have given any one permission to take out the car without telling me of it. I hastened up to the engine-house; but it was empty, and added nothing to my meagre stock of ideas on the vexed subject. The dummy was gone, and that was all I knew about it.

The Institute buildings were only a short distance from the engine-house, and I next went there in search of information. The students were engaged, in large numbers, in their sports. Indeed, there were so many of them present that the suspicion I had entertained that some of the boys had gone on a lark in the dummy seemed to be disarmed. Still, a dozen or twenty of them would not be missed in the crowd, and it was possible that this number were in mischief, though I thought, if it were so, they had chosen a singular time of day for it.

The students were rung up in the morning at six o'clock; but, by a merciful provision of the governors of the Institute, the first hour was devoted to play, so that those who were behind time cheated themselves out of just so much sport. I was informed that only a few neglected to get up when the bell rang; and I commend this humane and cunning arrangement to other institutions troubled by the matutinal tardiness of students. The morning is favorable to bold schemes and active movements; and the more I thought of the matter, the more anxious I became to know whose places would be vacant at the breakfast table, at seven o'clock, when the bell rang for the morning meal.

I inquired for Faxon, and soon found him making a " home run " in a game of base ball. Before I had time to address him the breakfast bell rang;

and with a most surprising unanimity, all games
were instantly suspended — a fact which ought to
convince humanitarian educators that breakfast, dinner, and supper should immediately follow play, if
boys are to be taught habits of promptness. The
students rushed towards "Grub Hall," as the dining-
room was called; but, though Faxon had a good
appetite, I succeeded, with some difficulty, in inter-
cepting his headlong flight.

"What's the row, Wolf?" demanded he, glancing
at the open door through which the boys were filing
to the breakfast table, and possibly fearing that the
delay would involve an inferior piece of beefsteak.

"Are any of the fellows missing?" I asked.

"Not that I know of; but we can tell at the
table," replied he. "What's up?"

"The dummy is gone," I answered, mysteriously.

"Gone! Gone where?"

"I don't know. I saw her streaking it down the
road as if she had been shot off."

"Don't say a word about it; but hold on here
till I get my grub, and see who is missing," said
he, rushing into the building.

I did not understand what Faxon purposed to do; but I was willing to comply with the arrangement, in compassion for his stomach, if for no other reason. I had feared that my associate on the engine was concerned in the conspiracy to abstract the dummy, for I did not think any one else would be able to manage it. I was glad to find he had not engaged in the lark, and I wondered all the more who had the audacity to play with the machine. I walked over to a point on the Institute grounds which commanded a view of the Lake Shore for some distance; but I could see nothing of the dummy. Presently, Faxon, who had satisfied the cravings of his hunger in a remarkably short time, came out of the building.

"Briscoe and half a dozen other fellows are missing," said he.

"Briscoe!" I exclaimed; for he was the fellow who had invaded my quarters the night before, and declared he could handle the engine.

"He's a first-rate fellow, in the main, and I hope he isn't getting into any scrape," added Faxon, anxiously.

"I'm afraid he is. He is the fellow who has run away with the dummy."

"Don't say a word. I have permission to be out an hour, and we will see where they are. What can we do?"

"We can take one of the platform cars, and go after them."

"Come along; but don't say anything."

We went to the engine-house, and lifted one of the platform cars on the track. The Lake Shore Railroad, as I had found by running the dummy, had a slight descent from Middleport to Spangleport. We pushed the car, running behind it, till we had worked it up to a high rate of speed, and then leaped upon the platform. The impetus thus given to it kept it going for a mile, when the motive power was applied again, as before. In this manner we ran three miles, without making very hard work of it, and came in sight of the dummy.

"There she is!" exclaimed Faxon. "The fellows did not go a great way in her."

"No! but they went as far as they could," I replied, as soon as I had examined the situation of the car, which was not in motion when we discovered it.

"How do you know?"

"She's off the track."

"That's too bad!"

For my own part I was rather glad the enterprise of the runaways had been nipped in the bud, for I had a professional contempt for those who attempt to run an engine when they know nothing about one. I only hoped the dummy and the boys were not injured. As we approached nearer to the scene of the disaster, we saw the conspirators hard at work trying to get the dummy on the track.

"What are you about, you spoonies!" shouted Faxon, as we stopped the car close to the unfortunate dummy.

"We are trying to get the thing on the track," replied Briscoe, as coolly as though he had done nothing wrong.

"How came she out here?" demanded Faxon.

"Oh, well, we were having a little fun with her."

"You were missed at breakfast, and you will catch fits for this."

" I suppose we shall; but we can't help it now."

" What did you meddle with her for, you spoonies, when you didn't know anything about her?" continued Faxon, indignantly.

" I know all about her, as well as you do, Faxon. You needn't put on airs because you helped run the thing," retorted Briscoe.

" I should think you did know all about her; and that's the reason why you ran her off the track. You don't know so much as you think you do."

" That may be, but I know more than you think I do."

" What did you run her off for?"

" I suppose it is considered rather necessary to have rails for this thing to run on," replied Briscoe. " If you will look ahead of her, you will see that the track is torn up for a quarter of a mile, and the rails carried off."

" Is that so?" added Faxon, walking out ahead of the dummy.

" That's so, as you may see for yourself," said Briscoe, following us along the track.

17

" Who did it? That's the next question," asked Faxon, vexed, as we all were, at the discovery.

" I don't know; we didn't," answered Briscoe. " If the track hadn't been pulled up, we should have returned at breakfast time. What's to be done?"

" You must get back as quick as you can," replied the benevolent Faxon. " I won't blow on you. Take that car, and make time for the Institute."

" You're a good fellow, Faxon," added Briscoe, with a smile.

" If I am, don't you play this game again."

" I won't, again."

" How did it work?" I inquired, wishing to hear the experience of the runaways.

" First rate. I had no trouble with it. She started when I pulled the thing, and we made time on her coming down, you had better believe."

" I should think you did. I saw you putting her through by daylight."

" Edwards saw the track was gone, and told me of it. I shut off steam, and put on the brakes; but I couldn't fetch up soon enough to keep from running off."

"All I have to say is, that you are lucky to come out of it with a whole skin," I added, solemnly. "But hurry back as fast as you can, or you will be in hot water."

"I'm in hot water now, and I may as well be scalded with a quart as a pint. I am willing to stay and help you put her on the track."

"Don't do it, Briscoe," interposed Faxon. "You are one of the directors, and if the major finds out you meddled with the dummy, he will have you turned out of office. Rush back to the Institute, and don't let on."

The runaways were willing to adopt this advice. There were half a dozen of them, and as they could make easy work of pushing the car back, they soon disappeared behind the trees.

"You won't let on — will you, Wolf?" said Faxon, in a coaxing tone, as soon as we were alone.

"I won't volunteer to tell any stories out of school; but I shall not tell any lies about it."

"Don't be squeamish. Briscoe is a good fellow, and one of the directors. The major would break him if he heard of this thing."

" Between you and me, I think he ought to be broken. Suppose they had burst the boiler, and been wiped out themselves ? "

" That's all very pretty ; but they didn't burst the boiler, and were not wiped out."

" I'm at work for Major Toppleton. If he asks me any questions, I shall tell him the truth."

" Oh, come now ! "

" But I don't think he is likely to ask me any questions. There will be a breeze when he finds out the track has been torn up, and there will be fog enough with it to cover up those fellows."

" Be a good fellow, Wolf, and don't say a word."

" I will not if I can help it. I don't think anybody will know anything about this scrape. Those who saw the dummy come out will suppose I was on her. But here's a pretty kettle of fish ! " I added, glancing at the dummy, and then at the road minus the rails.

" Can we put the thing on the track again ? "

" I think we can — we can try it, at least. We want some of those rails for levers."

"Where are they?" asked the puzzled Faxon. "Did some one steal them for old iron?"

"No; they are not far off," I replied, leading the way down to the Lake Shore.

We walked along the beach, till I discovered foot-steps in the sand.

"Here is where they landed," I added, pointing to the prints, and also to some deep lines gored in the sand by a couple of boats, which had been hauled up on the beach.

"Who landed? I don't understand it."

"I do; an enemy has done this. The Wimple-tonians have been over here during the night and torn up your track."

"If they did, it will be a sorry day for them," said Faxon, grating his teeth and shaking his head.

"These footprints were made by dandy boots, and all the party were boys. It's as plain as the nose on Colonel Wimpleton's face;" and the great man of Centreport was troubled with a long proboscis.

"They'll catch it for this."

We walked along till we came to Grass Brook, and there we found the rails thrown into the deep water at the mouth of it. The end of one of them lay within my reach, and I pulled it out. Using this as a lever, we pried up the wheels of the dummy, and, after an hour of severe exertion, we succeeded in putting the car upon the track.

CHAPTER XXIV.

THE GRAND PICNIC.

IT is not necessary for me to quote any of the big words which Major Toppleton used when I told him the Wimpletonians had been over and torn up a quarter of a mile of the track of the Lake Shore Railroad. I did not deem it best, as he asked no questions, to augment his wrath by telling him the dummy had been off the track. He was more impatient, if possible, to have the road completed than the boys were. He procured the services of a score of mechanics and laborers, and we hastened with them to the dismantled portion of the road. The rails were fished up from the deep water, and before twelve o'clock the track was in as good order as ever.

If the students of the Wimpleton Institute looked over the lake, and enjoyed the mischief they had done, — as of course they did, — their satisfaction was of short duration. Before they were turned out to play in the afternoon, the dummy was running her regular trips to Spangleport. I have no doubt the rascals who did the mischief felt cheap and crest-fallen when they saw the car going on its way as though nothing had happened ; and I had no more doubt that they would consider their work ill done, and attempt to do it over again. They were not allowed to go out nights ; but I am afraid the authorities of the Institute did not punish them very severely when they broke through the rules in order to do mischief to the establishment on the other side. It was only following the example of the magnate of Centreport and many of their elders ; and " like master, like man."

When the torn-up track was relaid, the twenty men were conveyed beyond Spangleport to build the road. Frogs and switches had been procured, the turning apparatus was finished, and I had the pleas-ure of running both ways in ship-shape style. By laying a few rods of track, and putting down a couple of switches near the engine-house, we were enabled to turn at the Middleport end. We always switched off to run into the engine-house, and we had to back in, from a point *above* the house. On the new track we ran out to a point *below*, and came upon the main line headed towards Spangleport. I take the more pride in describing these movements, because they were of my own invention, though I have since learned that similar plans had been used before.

Towards night on the second day of my railroad experience, Major Toppleton was a passenger in the engine-room. He was in high spirits to think the mischief done by the Wimpletonians had been so speedily repaired; but he was afraid the daring act would be repeated, as I was quite satisfied it would. I knew my late comrades on the Centreport side well enough to understand that they would never let the Lake Shore Railroad enjoy peace and prosperity until they were provided with an equivalent. I was confident that Colonel Wimpleton was racking his brains even then for a scheme which would produce an equal excitement among the students of his Institute.

"You know those villains over there better than I do, Wolf," said the major confidentially to me; and I was amazed to hear him own that I knew anything better than he did. "Don't you think they will attempt to tear up the track again?"

"Yes, sir, I do think so," I replied.

"The rascals! It mortifies me to have them get ahead of me in this manner. If I could only catch them, I would cure them of night wandering very quick. It is of no use for me to complain to the colonel, or to the principal of the Wimpleton Institute. They would enjoy my chagrin."

"It is easy enough to prevent them from doing any more mischief," I added.

"How?" he asked, eagerly.

"By setting a watch."

"Yes; and while we are watching in one place they will tear up the rails in another."

"There are two ways to do it. Your tow-boat can ply up and down the shore, or we can run the dummy all night."

"Do you think you can stand it to run the dummy all night, Wolf?" laughed he.

" My father and I could for a few nights."

The tow-boat had gone up the lake with a fleet of canal boats, and the other plan was the only alternative. I saw my father at six o'clock. He was ready to serve on the watch, but he was not willing to leave my mother alone with my sisters at home all night, fearful that some of the chivalrous Wimpletonians might undertake to annoy her. But Faxon volunteered to serve with me, and was pleased with the idea. We lighted up the reflecting lamp over the door of the engine, and, though it was dark, we put her " through by daylight," in a figurative sense.

We talked till we were sleepy, and then by turns each of us took a nap, lying upon the cushions of the passenger compartment. It was a good bed, and we enjoyed the novelty of the situation. Faxon by this time understood the machinery very well, and I was not afraid to trust him. We did not run on regular hours, and lay still more than half the time, after Faxon had run the car as much as he desired. We kept an eye on the lake for boats, of which the Wimpletonians had a whole squadron.

Only once during the night was there anything like an alarm. We saw half a dozen boats come down through the Narrows about eleven o'clock, but we soon lost sight of them under the shadow of the opposite shore. We saw nothing more of them, and I concluded that the dummy, with her bright light on the shore, had prevented another attack upon the railroad. After this all was quiet, and there was nothing to get up an excitement upon.

The next day I was rather sleepy at times, and so was Faxon. At eight o'clock the major appeared, and I told him we had probably prevented another raid upon the road, for we had seen a fleet of boats pass through the Narrows.

"All right, Wolf; I am glad we balked the scoundrels," answered the major; and almost anything seemed to be a victory to the great man of Middleport.

"I suppose they will try again some other time," I added.

"We will see that they don't succeed. Now we must push along the road as fast as we can. I don't like to disappoint the boys, but I can't wait for them to build the rest of it."

I could not help smiling.

"What is it, Wolf?" he asked, smiling with me; and great men's smiles are sunshine to the heart.

"I don't think they will cry if you don't let them do any more."

"Don't you? Why, they begged me to let them do the work with their own hands, and I have gratified them thus far."

I soon convinced him that the boys were not anxious to do any more digging, or to lay any more rails; that hard work was "played out" with them. The magnate was delighted to hear it; and there was no grumbling because the students were not called upon to use the shovels and the hammers. I ran the dummy out with the men, after that, every morning at seven o'clock, and the road progressed rapidly towards Grass Springs.

At noon we heard astounding news from Centreport. All the boats belonging to the Wimpleton Institute — not less than a dozen of them — had mysteriously disappeared. No one knew what had happened to them, and no one had heard anything in the night to indicate what had become of them. Major Toppleton inquired very particularly about the fleet of boats Faxon and I had seen; but our information did not elucidate the mystery. I observed that my fellow-engineer winked at me very significantly, as though he knew more than he chose to tell.

"What did you wink for, Faxon?" I asked, when we started on our trip, and were alone.

"You are blind as the major," laughed he.

"What do you mean?"

"About forty of the Toppletonians found a way to get out of the Institute last night. You won't say a word about this — will you?"

"You had better not tell me, Faxon."

"But I will tell you, for I don't think the major or the principal will say anything if the whole thing is blown. You know where the quarries are, above Centreport, on that side."

"Of course I do."

"The Wimpleton boats, loaded with rocks, and the plugs taken out, lie at the bottom of the lake, in twenty feet of water, off the quarries. We are even with those fellows now for tearing up our track."

"That's too bad!" I exclaimed.

"Too bad! It wasn't too bad to tear up our track — was it?" replied he, indignantly.

"Two wrongs don't make a right," I replied, sagely.

"But one evil sometimes corrects another — '*similia similibus curantur*,' as our little-pill doctor used to say. The loss of their boats will prevent the Wimps from coming over here again in the night to cut up our road."

I was a boy, like the rest of them; but I did not exactly enjoy this "tit for tat" business. My mother had always taught me to exercise a Christian spirit, and this "paying back" was a diabolical spirit. I would not tell of these things, nor suffer my readers to gloat over them, if any are disposed to do so — were it not to show how these two great men, and all the little men who hung upon the skirts of their coats, were finally reconciled to each other; and how, out of war and vengeance, came "peace and good will to men."

Before Miss Grace Toppleton's birthday arrived the road was finished to Sandy Beach, and the grand picnic took place. The two platform cars had seats built upon them, and were attached to the dummy. I conveyed about a hundred a trip until the middle of the day, when all Middleport appeared to have been transported to the grove. The affair was very elaborate in all its details. Tents, pavilions, booths, and swings had been erected, and the Ucayga Cornet Band was on the ground.

When I came in on the twelve o'clock trip, my father presented himself at the door of the engine-room, his face wreathed in smiles. My mother and sisters were present, for we were now regarded as Middleporters.

"I will take care of this thing for a short time, Wolf, and you may go and see the fun," said my father.

"I don't care about going now."

"Oh, you must go; the people want to see you."

Thus urged I entered the grove, and found my-

self before a speaker's stand, on which Major Toppleton was holding forth to the people.

"Come here, Wolf!" called he. "I want to see
you."

A couple of the students seized me by the arms,
and, dragging me forward, actually forced me up the
steps upon the speaker's stand. I blushed, was bewildered and confused.

"Three cheers for Wolf!" shouted Faxon; and
they were given.

"Come forward, Wolf. The people want to see
you," added the major, dragging me to the front of
the stage.

I blushed, and tried to escape; and then the great
man jumped down, and left me alone on the platform.
I took off my cap, and bowed.

"Mr. Wolf."

I turned. Miss Grace Toppleton was on the stage
with me. I looked at her with wonder.

"Mr. Wolf," she continued, "the students of the
Toppleton Institute, grateful to you for your labors
on the Lake Shore Railroad, wish to present you

18

this gold watch; and I assure you it affords me very great pleasure to be the bearer of this token to you."

She handed me the watch, and I took it, with a red face and a trembling hand.

WLC.

THE GIFT OF THE TOPPLETONIANS. — Page 274.

CHAPTER XXV.

WOLF'S SPEECH.

I WAS never so "taken aback" in my life as when I heard the silvery voice of Miss Grace Toppleton, and saw the magnificent gift in her hand. At any time I should have looked at her with interest; but just then it seemed to me that the sun had ceased to shine, and all the light which flowed down upon the brilliant scene around me came from her beautiful face. I wished there was a hole in the platform beneath me, through which I might sink out of sight; but then, I am sure, if I had gone down into the gloom of the space beneath me, I should instantly have wished myself back again; for I was the hero of the occasion, and the soft eyes of Miss Grace were fixed upon me.

As I listened to the silvery tones of the fair orator, I became conscious that I was presenting a

very awkward appearance. My hands seemed to
be as big as the feet of an elephant, and altogether
too large to go into my pockets. I did not know
what to do with them, or where to put them. I
felt like a great clumsy booby. But when the
thought flashed upon me that Miss Grace was looking at me, and that she must consider me a boor-
ish cub, I felt the necessity of doing something
to redeem myself. When I was fully conscious that
she was observing me, I quite forget that anybody
else was engaged in a similar occupation. I straight-
ened up, stiffened the quaking muscles in my frame,
and permitted my cumbrous hands to fall at my
side, just as the professor of elocution in the Wimpleton Institute had instructed me to do when I
spoke " in public on the stage."

If the change of attitude produced no effect upon
others, it did in me, for I knew then that I looked
like a civilized boy, and bore myself with the dignity
becoming the young engineer of the Lake Shore
Railroad. Miss Grace handed me the watch, and
I took it with my best bow. She finished her
" neat little speech," and, as her silvery tones ceased,

I was painfully conscious that something was expected of me. It was a hard case. Clinging to the cow-catcher of a locomotive going at thirty miles an hour was nothing to it. Again I longed for a hole in the platform through which I might disappear from the public gaze. But there was no hole in the platform, and no chance to escape. The audience were heartily applauding the presentation speech of Miss Grace; and I think the major was prouder of her then than he had ever before been in his life.

While this demonstration was in progress, I tried to gather up my thoughts for the mighty effort I was to make. A labored apology, with something about being in a "tight place," flashed upon my mind as a suitable preface to my speech; but I almost as quickly decided not to make any apology; for, since no one could suspect me of being a speech-maker, I was not likely to fall below their expectations as an orator. Before I had concluded what I should say, or try to say, the applause ceased for an instant, and then the Toppletonians began to shout, "Speech! Speech!"

If I could run an engine, there was no good reason why I should not make a speech. I had something to say, and all I had to do was to say it. Really it seemed to be the simplest thing in the world, and I determined to "go in," however I might come out of it. In a word, I was resolved to put it "through by daylight."

"Miss Grace Toppleton," I began, and the uttering of the whole name seemed to afford me a grateful respite of some fraction of a second in which to gather up the next idea. "I am very much obliged to the students of the Toppleton Institute for this beautiful gift. A gold watch is something I never expected to have. I didn't think of anything of this kind when I came in here, and for that reason I was very much surprised. I shall always keep this watch, and, whenever I look at its face, it will remind me of the generous fellows who gave it to me. I shall" —

I was interrupted by a burst of rapturous applause from the students; and while I was waiting for it to subside, I was satisfied that I was doing very well.

"I shall endeavor, with the help of this watch, always to be on time; and I hope I shall be able to do my duty to the officers and to ⁻the liberal patron of the Lake Shore Railroad. Miss Topple-ton, I am very grateful to all the good fellows who have given me this splendid watch; and though I don't believe in wearing two faces, I shall never look at the face of this watch without thinking of another face — the face of the one who so prettily presented it."

"Good! Good!" shouted the students; and an-other round of applause encouraged me in my arduous task.

"I shall always prize this watch," I continued, glancing at the beautiful time-keeper, "for the sake of those who gave it to me; and I am sure I shall give it a double value because of the fair hands from which it passed into my own. With ten thousand thanks for the beautiful gift, I shall try to perform my duty better than ever before; and whatever work is given me to do, I shall put it through by daylight."

I made my best bow again, and retired from the

stage amid a storm of applause. As Miss Grace followed me, I helped her down the steps. The pleasant, arch smile she bestowed upon me made me feel that I had not said anything which she disliked.

"Mr. Wolf, you are quite a speech-maker," said she.

"I don't know; I never did any such thing before," I replied, blushing like a little girl.

"You did it real well, Mr. Wolf; and when they don't want you to run the engine, you must go to Congress."

"If I had only known what was going on, I should have got ready for it, and shouldn't have felt quite so sheepish."

"That would have spoiled the whole. You did splendidly. Now let me fasten the chain to your vest, and see how you look with the watch on."

She took the watch from my hand, adjusted the chain in a button-hole of my vest with her own fair hands, and I could hardly resist the temptation to do or say something intensely ridiculous; but I did resist it, and only thanked her as coolly as I could for the service. Major Toppleton came up and congratulated me on my speech. I think they did not expect me to be able to say anything, and perhaps some of the students would have enjoyed the scene quite as much if I had broken down completely. But I am confident that all the compliments I received were based upon the very meagre expectations of my intelligent audience.

The students used me very handsomely, and for the time did not put on any airs. They treated me as an equal, and even Tommy Toppleton was as gracious as though I had been the scion of a great house like his own. Miss Grace walked with me to the refreshment tables, and while the band, whose leader seemed to be an awful satirist, wickedly played, " Hail to the Chief," I partook of chicken salad, cake, and ice-cream, being actually waited upon by the fair oratorical divinity who had presented me the watch. I was afraid she would scold me for saying that I should think of her face whenever I looked at the face of the watch; but she did not, and I suppose she regarded the daring expression as a piece of " buncombe " tolerated by the license of such an occasion.

I spent an hour in the most agreeable manner in the Sandy Beach Grove; indeed, the whole scene is still a bright spot in my memory. But I was obliged to return to the dummy, for after all I was only a poor boy, an employee of the magnate of Toppleton. I was out of place at the feast and the revel; but I was very grateful to the students, and to all the people, especially Miss Grace Toppleton, who had treated me with such "distinguished consideration." I resumed my place on the engine, and as there were a great many people to convey back to Middleport, I made quick trips, and literally succeeded in putting them all "through by daylight."

After I had put up the dummy for the night, I went over to Centreport with my father, mother, and sisters in the major's sail-boat, which he placed at my disposal for the purpose. I had never seen my parents so happy before. If they were proud of me, I could afford to forgive them for it. We had almost forgotten that the cloud of misfortune had ever lowered above us. My father had not tasted a drop of liquor since the fatal day on which he had lost his money, and this was enough to make us all happy, without any of the other pleasant events which had gladdened our hearts. God had been very merciful to us, and had turned the wrath of man into blessings for us, and I am sure we were all grateful to him for his goodness.

Nothing definite had been heard from Christy Holgate, but it was believed that he had gone to the South. A close watch was kept upon his family in Ucayga; for it was supposed that he would send for them, and it was hoped that their movements would enable the officer in charge of the case to ascertain his present residence. My father despaired of ever hearing from the runaway or the money, and all agreed that it would be but a poor satisfaction to have the wretch sent to the state prison for even a short term.

We walked from the mill wharf up to the house after I had securely moored the sail-boat. We were still talking over the pleasant events of the day, and for the third time I had showed my watch to my sisters, who were prouder of it than I was.

As we approached the house, I saw Captain Synders sitting on the fence, and apparently waiting for the return of my father or myself. I could not believe that he had any business with me, for Colonel Wimpleton had paid the honest skipper for the destruction of his boat, and nothing had been said for a week about arresting me for taking part in the mischief.

"I'm waiting for you, Mr. Penniman," said Synders, as we went up to the gate.

"I hope you haven't had to wait long," replied my father, gently.

"Long enough," added the constable, gruffly.

"What can I do for you?" inquired my father, rather anxiously, I thought, though his face wore a good-natured smile.

"Nothing for me, but you can do something for Colonel Wimpleton."

"What can I do for him?"

"Pay the note of two thousand dollars which was due at noon to-day," continued Synders, maliciously.

"Colonel Wimpleton knows very well that my

money was stolen from me, and that I cannot pay him," replied my father.

"It's nothing to him that your money was stolen. You must pay the note."

"I can't do that."

"Well, we know you didn't do it, and this afternoon the colonel foreclosed the mortgage. I'm here to give you notice of it, and to warn you out of the house."

"Does he mean to turn me out to-night?" asked my father.

"I shall give you legal notice to quit, before witnesses."

"I will pay rent for the house," suggested my father.

"That won't do," answered Synders, shaking his head. "The house must be sold after legal notice has been given; and in my opinion it won't bring a dollar over the mortgage, under the hammer."

"Well, I can't help myself," added my father, gloomily.

"You made a bad mistake when you turned upon the colonel," sneered the officer.

"I didn't turn upon him; but we will not talk about that."

My father was very much depressed at the thought of losing the thousand dollars which he had invested in his house. All he had saved was to be swept away from him. The constable procured his witnesses, served his legal notices, and went away chuckling over the misery he left behind him. Doubtless he exaggerated the confusion and dismay of my father when he reported his doings to his employer, and the great man gloated proportionally over the wreck he was making.

CHAPTER XXVI.

THE AUCTION SALE.

MY father was very unhappy, and my mother was afraid he would again resort to the cup for solace in his misfortune. I do not know what she said to him; but he treated her very tenderly, and never was a woman more devoted than she was during this threatening misfortune. My father was again a poor man. All that he had of worldly goods was to be stripped from him to satisfy the malice of his hard creditor. He was too proud to apply to Major Toppleton for assistance, believing that he would have nothing to do with property on the other side of the lake.

I continued to run the dummy, and was so happy as to keep on the right side of the major, his son, and the students. Before the expiration of the legal notice, my father hired a small house in Middleport, and we moved into it. It was only a hovel, compared with the neat and comfortable dwelling we had occupied in Centreport, and the change was depressing to all the members of the family. My father's place was advertised to be sold, and as the day — which looked like a fatal one to us — drew near, we were all very sad and nervous. Nothing had yet been heard of Christy; and the case was a plain one. The thousand dollars saved from the earnings of the debtor was to be sacrificed. No man in Centreport, however much he wanted the house, would dare to bid upon it.

My father desired to attend the sale, perhaps hopeful that his presence might induce some friend of other days to bid a little more for the place. My mother did not wish to have him attend the auction; but as he insisted, she desired that I should go with him. I had no wish to be present at the humiliating spectacle, or to endure the sneers and the jeers of the Centreporters; but I decided to go, for my presence might be some restraint upon my father, if his misfortunes tempted him to drink again. I applied to Major Toppleton for leave of absence for my father and myself on the day of the sale. My father had engaged a man to take his place, and Faxon could now run the dummy.

"What's going on over there?" asked the major, after he had consented to the absence of both of us.

"My father's place is to be sold at auction. Colonel Wimpleton has foreclosed the mortgage," I replied.

"How much has your father paid on the house?"

"He paid a thousand dollars down; and the mortgage is for two thousand. He would have paid the note when it was due, but his money was stolen from him."

"I remember about that," added the major, musing. "Will the place bring enough at auction to enable your father to get back the thousand dollars he paid?"

"No, sir; we don't expect it will bring anything over the mortgage. Colonel Wimpleton means to punish my father by ruining him, and none of the Centreport people will dare to bid on the place."

He asked me several questions more, and I told him as well as I could how the matter stood. I was hoping most earnestly that he would offer to advance the money to pay off the mortgage; but just as my expectations reached the highest pitch, a gentleman interrupted the conversation, and the major went off with him in a few moments, having apparently forgotten all about the subject. My hopes were dashed down. I conveyed all the students out to Sandy Beach in the dummy that afternoon, and brought them back; but I was so absorbed in our family affairs that I hardly knew what I was doing.

At one o'clock the next day, I went over to Centreport with father to attend the sale. He was very nervous, and I was hardly less so. At the appointed time, a large collection of people gathered around the house. A red flag was flying on the fence, and all the company seemed as jovial as if they were assembled for a picnic, rather than to complete the ruin of my poor father. Hardly any one spoke to us; but I saw many who appeared to be talking about us, and enjoying the misery we experienced at the prospect of seeing our beloved home pass into other hands.

Colonel Wimpleton was there, and so was Waddie. Both of them seemed to be very happy, and both of them stared at us as though we had no right to set foot on the sacred soil of Centreport. Others imitated their illustrious example, and we were made as uncomfortable as possible. In our hearing, and evidently for our benefit, a couple of men discussed their proposed bids, one declaring that he would go as high as fifteen dollars, while the other would not be willing to take the place at so high a figure. Finally, the colonel, after passing us a dozen times, halted before my father.

"I suppose you have come over to bid on the place, Ralph," said he.

"No, sir; I have nothing to back my bid with," replied my father, meekly.

"You had better bid; I don't think it will bring more than fifteen or twenty dollars over the mortgage," chuckled the magnate.

"It ought to bring fifteen hundred," added my father. "I was offered that for it once."

"You should have taken it. Real estate is very much depressed in the market."

" I should think it was; and I'm afraid Centre-port is going down," answered my father, with a faint smile.

" Going down! " exclaimed the great man, stung by the reflection. "Any other piece of property in Centreport would sell a hundred per cent. higher than this."

" I suppose so! " ejaculated my poor father, fully understanding the reason why his place was to be sacrificed.

The auctioneer, who had mounted the steps of the front door, interrupted the conversation. He stated that he was about to sell all the right, title, and interest which Ralph Penniman had in the estate at twelve o'clock on a certain day, described the mortgage, and called for a bid.

" Twenty-five cents," said a colored man in the crowd.

The audience gave way to a hearty burst of laughter at the richness of the bid.

" Thirty cents," added Colonel Wimpleton, as soon as the noise had subsided.

The auctioneer dwelt on it for a moment, and

then the colored man advanced to thirty-one cents. By this time it was clear to us that these proceedings were a farce, intended to torment my father. I had never endured agonies more keen than those which followed these ridiculous bids, as I became conscious that my father was the butt of the company's derision. The colonel, more liberal than the negro, went up to thirty-five cents; whereupon the latter advanced another cent, amid the laughter and jeers of the assembly. Thus it continued for some time, the colored man, who had doubtless been engaged to play his part, going up one cent and the great man four. Others occasionally bid a cent or a half-cent more; and half an hour was consumed in windy eloquence by the auctioneer, and in cent and half-cent bids, before the offer reached a dollar.

"One dollar and five cents," said Colonel Wimpleton, at this point.

"One dollar and six cents," promptly responded the negro.

"One dollar and six cents is bid for this very desirable estate," added the auctioneer. "Consider, gentlemen, the value of this property, and the circumstances under which it is sold. Every dollar you bid goes into the pocket of the honest and hard-working mortgagor."

"One dollar and ten cents," said the colonel, as if moved by this appeal.

"Dollar 'leven," added the negro.

"Consider, gentlemen, the situation of the unfortunate man whose interest in this property I am selling."

"Dollar fifteen," said the colonel.

"Dollar fifteen and a half," persisted the negro, amid roars of laughter.

"One thousand dollars," said some one in the rear of the crowd, in a loud, clear tone.

If the explosion of the honest skipper's canal boat, which had been the indirect cause of the present gathering, had taken place in the midst of the crowd, it could not have produced greater amazement and consternation than the liberal bid of the gentleman on the outskirts of the assemblage. It was a bombshell of the first magnitude which burst upon the hilarious people of Centreport, met, as it seemed to me, for the sole purpose of sacrificing my poor father. I recognized the voice of the bidder.

It was Major Toppleton.

I had not seen him before. I did not know he was present. I afterwards learned that he arrived only a moment before he made the bid, and only had time to perceive the nature of the farce which was transpiring before he turned it into a tragedy.

" Dollar fifteen and a half," repeated the auctioneer, so startled that he chose not to take the astounding bid of the magnate of Middleport.

" I bid one thousand dollars," shouted Major Toppleton, angrily, as he forced his way through the crowd to the foot of the steps where the auctioneer stood.

" One thousand dollars is bid," said the auctioneer, reluctantly.

I looked at Colonel Wimpleton, who stood near me. His face was red, and his portly frame quaked with angry emotions. My father's property in the house was saved. We looked at each other, and smiled our gratitude.

"Toppleton must not have the property," said Colonel Wimpleton to his lawyer, who stood next to him, while his teeth actually grated with the

savage ire which shook his frame. "He will put a
nuisance under my very nose. Eleven hundred,"
gasped the great man of Centreport, with frantic
energy; and he was so furious at the interference
of the major that I do not think he knew what he
was about.

"Twelve hundred," added Major Toppleton, quietly,
now that this bid had been taken.

"Thirteen," hoarsely called the colonel.

"Fourteen."

"Fifteen."

The crowd stood with their mouths wide open,
waiting the issue with breathless eagerness. The
auctioneer repeated the bids as he would have pro-
nounced the successive sentences of his own death
warrant. Colonel Wimpleton had by this time forgotten all about my father, and was intent only on
preventing his great enemy from buying the estate.

"Sixteen," said the major, who, seeing the torture
he was inflicting upon his malignant rival, was in
excellent humor.

"Seventeen," promptly responded Colonel Wimpleton.

" Eighteen."

" Nineteen," gasped the colonel.

" Two thousand."

" Twenty-one hundred," roared the colonel, desperately.

" Twenty-two," laughed the major.

The colonel was listening to the remonstrance of his lawyer, and the auctioneer was permitted to dwell on the last bid for a moment.

" Twenty-three ! " shouted the colonel.

" Twenty - three hundred dollars — twenty - three, twenty-three, twenty-three," chipped the auctioneer, with professional formality, when the major did not instantly follow the last bid. " Going at twenty-three hundred ! Are you all done ? "

" Knock it off ! " growled the colonel, savagely, but in a low tone.

" Going at twenty-three hundred — one — two — three — and gone, to Colonel Wimpleton, at twenty-three hundred," added the auctioneer, as he brought down his hammer for the last time.

" Pretty well sold, after all," said the major to me, as he rubbed his hands.

"Yes, sir; thanks to you, it is very well sold," I replied, running over with joy at the unexpected termination of the farce.

Colonel Wimpleton swore like a pirate. He was the maddest man on the western continent.

"Colonel, if you are dissatisfied with your bargain, I shall be happy to take the property at my last bid," said the major as he walked out into the road.

I will not repeat what the great man of Centre-port said in reply, for it was not fit to be set down on clean, white paper. My father and I crossed the lake, and went home with the good news to my mother, who was anxiously waiting to hear the result. Whatever joy she experienced at the good fortune of my father, she was too good a woman to exult over the quarrels of the two great men.

"I think Colonel Wimpleton will not try to punish me any more," said my father. "He pays eight hundred dollars more than I was offered for the place. If he is satisfied, I am."

The next day the twenty-three hundred dollars, less the expenses of the sale, was paid over to my father. He had already cast longing eyes upon a beautiful estate on the outskirts of the town of Middleport, having ten acres of land, with a fine orchard; but the owner would not sell it for less than five thousand dollars. The fruit upon the place would more than pay the interest of the money; and, as soon as he had received the proceeds of the sale, he bought the estate, paying two thousand down, and giving a mortgage for three thousand. We moved in immediately. The house was even better than that we had occupied in Centreport, and I assure the reader, in concluding my story, that we were as happy as any family need be left at the end of a last chapter.

Of the Lake Shore Railroad I have much more to say, in other stories which will follow. The road was soon completed to Grass Springs, thirteen miles from Middleport, and I ran the dummy to that point during the autumn. In due time we had a regular locomotive and cars, and ran to Ucayga, where we connected with a great line of railway between the east and the west. We had a great deal of trouble with the Wimpletonians, and the

Centreporters generally, of which something will be said in my next story — "LIGHTNING EXPRESS, OR THE RIVAL ACADEMIES."

The Toppletonians continued to treat me very kindly, and I did my best for them. Our family troubles appeared to be all ended. My father was as steady as he had ever been, and though we heard nothing from Christy, we were on the high road to prosperity. Miss Grace Toppleton was frequently a passenger in the dummy, and I must add that she was always very kind and considerate to me. I am sure her smile encouraged me to be good and true, and to be faithful in the discharge of my duty; or, in other words, to put it THROUGH BY DAYLIGHT.